- Etisalat Prize for Literatu
- *Sunday Times* Barry Ronge Ficti

One of the Best Books of the Year
—*City Press, The Sunday Times, The Star, This is Africa, Africa's a Country, Sunday World*

"Ntshanga offers a devastating story yet tells it with noteworthy glow and flow that keeps pages turning until the glimmer-of-hope ending."
—LIBRARY JOURNAL

"With a fine lyricism of style Ntshanga weaves a story both filled with ennui and weird purpose. And if that sounds unlikely, it is a feat he pulls off with brilliance. The shining point of this novel is the author's ability to create the confusion and changes young South Africans have to deal with. In a modern state there are calls and cries from the past that still make claims on them. Never preachy or pretentious, this book is a breath of fresh air in an often fetid landscape. Read it, savor the beauty of the writing, and you will find yourself drawn into a dreamscape you may recognize."
—THE NEW AGE

"From time to time a novel comes along that is so strange, yet so utterly fresh and compelling, that it feels tuned into a reality with which you are not yet familiar."
—AERODROME

"One of [Ntshanga's] best qualities as a writer is to defamiliarize aspects of South African existence, which through our habits of speaking and writing, have boiled down to bland indifference… *The Reactive* will probably remain, along with Imraan Coovadia's *High Low In-between* and Jonny Steinberg's *Three Letter Plague*, as a seminal work confronting [a] period in our country's history."
—THE SUNDAY INDEPENDENT

"Elegiac… an astoundingly brilliant novel, radiating with understanding and compassion. It fulfills William Faulkner's injunction that 'the poet's voice need not merely be the record of man; it can be one of the props, the pillars to help him endure and prevail.'"
—CITY PRESS

THE REACTIVE

a novel by

MASANDE NTSHANGA

Two Dollar Radio
Books too loud to Ignore

TWO DOLLAR RADIO is a family-run outfit founded in 2005 with the mission to reaffirm the cultural and artistic spirit of the publishing industry.

We aim to do this by presenting bold works of literary merit, each book, individually and collectively, providing a sonic progression that we believe to be too loud to ignore.

Two Dollar Radio
Books too loud to Ignore

COLUMBUS, OHIO
For more information visit us here:
TwoDollarRadio.com

The Reactive by Masande Ntshanga was published in slightly different form in 2014 in South Africa by Penguin Random House South Africa's Umuzi imprint.

Copyright © 2016 by Masande Ntshanga
All rights reserved
ISBN: 978-1-937512-43-9
Library of Congress Control Number available upon request.

Author photograph: Simiato
Cover Illustrations: Pola Maneli
Design and layout: Two Dollar Radio

Printed on Enviro 100% post-consumer EcoLogo certified paper, processed chlorine free and manufactured using biogas energy.

100%   PERMANENT   **BIO GAS** ENERGY

Printed in Canada

"We need to look at the question that is posed, understandably I suppose: does HIV cause AIDS?"
—THABO MBEKI, FORMER PRESIDENT OF SOUTH AFRICA

"We are as forlorn as children lost in the woods."
—FRANZ KAFKA

THE REACTIVE

TEN YEARS AGO, I HELPED A HANDFUL OF MEN take my little brother's life. I wasn't there when it happened, but I told Luthando where to find them. Earlier that year, my brother and I had made a pact to combine our initiation ceremonies.

This was back in 1993.

LT was only seventeen then. He was broad of shoulder, but known as a wimp at Ngangelizwe High. My brother was good-looking in a funny way that never helped him any, and, like me, he was often called *ibhari*, or useless, by the older guys in the neighborhood. LT was bad with girls, too; most of them had decided against us pretty early. I don't know; maybe it's strange that I remember that about him most of all. I suppose my brother was handed the lousy luck of every guy in our family except our dad, who'd thrown us into different wombs one year after the other. We had cousins like that, too, all of them dealt a similar hand. In the end, it was winter when Luthando went to the hills to set things straight for himself. He went up thinking I would follow behind him.

It was raining when the *bakkie* took him on its back and drove him up the dirt trail. Inside the camp, they put him in line with a set of boys he shared a classroom with. Then they took out their blades. Afterwards, they nursed him for a week, and he kicked and swore at them for another two. They called him The

Screamer, they told us later, when we gathered to put him inside the earth. Maybe it was meant with tenderness, I thought, the kind of tenderness men could keep between themselves in the hills.

One morning, they said, my brother had failed to make the sounds they'd come to know him for. Luthando wasn't due out for another two days. The sky had been an empty blue expanse, easy on their duties around *eziko*, and they'd missed his peculiar fussiness. When they walked into his hut, one after the other, they found a memory instead of the man they were out to make. That was my little brother, LT, dead at seventeen, and I've never forgotten it was me who put him there.

I never went back home after we buried him. This isn't a story about me and my brother from the Transkei, about the Mda boys from eMthatha or the village of Qokolweni, where my grandmother's bones lie polished and buried next to her Ma's. Instead, I want to tell you about what happened to me in Cape Town after Luthando had taken his death. It's where I went to school and tried to make something of myself. It's also where I began to reconsider what my hands had made, and my telling of how it broke won't take us very long.

I went to college two times in my life. I might as well begin with how things went for me there. I first attended the university in Rondebosch, just up the road from the main strip, and when I'd dropped out of my journalism degree I enrolled at the technikon in town, where I got my science diploma and my sickness. I had an equity scholarship—there had been plenty of those to go around for whoever looked the way I did, back then. I got through on mostly average grades, too, like most of the guys in my class. When the year came to an end, there was a bunch of us who'd file into the Fees Office again to fill out all the forms required of boys who shared my skin tone. It didn't take much to go to school for free, in those days, or rather to trade on the pigment we were given to carry. I think I did all right, if you consider everything else, and I graduated with an upper-second-class pass in the end. I still have that diploma sitting somewhere in my flat in Observatory.

Now what else? In between university and Tech, I spent close to half a year at Bhut' Vuyo's place. Two weeks after dropping out of the university, I tried to go home, but I couldn't set foot inside my mother's house. The home I'd known since I was a child was barred to me. There could've been a tapestry of fire that flowed over each of our walls that day. In fact, thinking about it now, even that feels like an understatement.

My mother felt disgraced by my decision to leave the university and my bachelor's degree behind me in Rondebosch. It was too soon, she complained, first over the phone and then again in person. For a few moments, she even refused to turn her face up towards me. Instead, Ma arranged for me to enter the home of a relative.

Bhut' Vuyo was known as a great mechanic, a recovering alcoholic, and someone who'd been a doting stepfather to the little brother I'd helped to kill. He'd met my aunt, Sis' Funeka, when Luthando was only ten years old, and before then, sticking his hands into rusting bonnets had taken Bhut' Vuyo to Okinawa as a man of barely twenty. Pushed forward by the locomotive of a lucrative Toyota scholarship, he'd gone to the city of Kyoto at the age of twenty-four, before coming back and accepting too many drinks on the house in a tavern called Silver's. That was in Bisho, during the decline of the homeland years, and they'd served him on a cloth-covered tray every morning after he'd taken his table. It was no more than a month, people said, before my uncle was undone. There were decades that would nearly fell him after that: Bhut' Vuyo barely standing on his two feet around the neighborhood, and Bhut' Vuyo tottering on street corners next to the highway in Mdantsane. He was often seen with his toes busting out through the smiles on his black-and-blue gumboots, his head lolling as wispy as an old hornet's nest over his shoulders.

Now, my mother told me, having wrung himself dry, and maybe for good this time, Bhut' Vuyo lived with his second wife in Du Noon. They had two small children and her older son from a previous marriage, all of them born with bright eyes and strong teeth and each glowing with the promise of long-lasting health. For her part, my aunt had passed away shortly after we'd buried her son. Sis' Funeka had had a cancer eating away at her throat, and I suppose it had grown too impatient with the rigorous hold of her grief.

In the end, it had been a punishment for me to be sent to Du Noon, I had known that even then, but thinking of my little brother, of Luthando, I'd made myself accept the idea. And so I went to Du Noon like my mother wanted me to and ended up staying there for six months. I suppose some things happened when I was out there, too, and I drew close to those folks who'd taken me in. The subject of Luthando came up, as I thought it would, and in my gratitude to them, I made a promise to Bhut' Vuyo and his household.

Now, close to eight years later, I receive a text message from my uncle that reminds me of the words we shared back then, and of the promise I made, on a night so long ago I can hardly put it together from memory.

FIRST PART

THIS MORNING, WHEN I OPENED MY EYES, I FOUND another warm Saturday wrapping itself around the peninsula. Someone had left Cissie's living-room window open again, the one on the east-facing wall, above the copy of Rothko's *No. 4* that she'd painted for the three of us last week. Standing there in front of the glass, I couldn't tell you which one of us had left the window open, only that when I heard the wind blowing under the wooden sash again, I felt I was on my own here. There was a blanket of smog stretching itself thick over the rim of the metropolis, and everything looked inflated and exhausted all at once. I remembered all the different things inside this city, and how they changed the moment you got used to them. Then I remembered myself, too.

I closed the window after that, and soon my eyes followed.

Now it's a little later. Outside, the sky seems geared up for another humid weekend over the city, another three days of trees at war with their roots, and of dirty window panes getting stripped clean by the late winter rain.

I take a shallow breath.

Then cough.

Where I am right now is Newlands. I'm over at Cecelia's place, and I suppose the situation is easy enough to explain. It's still a long stretch of time before I die, but only three short hours since I received the message from my uncle, and everything's happening the way it usually does between me and my friends. Like always, the three of us—that's me, Ruan and Cecelia—we wake up some time before noon and take two Ibuprofens each. Then we go back to sleep, wake up an hour later, and take another two from the 800-milligram pack. Then Cissie turns on the stove to cook up a batch of glue, and the three of us wander around mutely after that, digging the sleep out of our eyes and caroming off each other's limbs. We drift through whatever passes for early afternoon here at Cissie's place.

This morning, I find my skin mottled with goose-flesh. I'm standing with one foot on cold chipped tile and the other on wet concrete. I'm yawning, still wiping stray motes from my eyes, and in a way, I guess these motes might be tears, but that's also me having my eyelids closed against that idea. That's also me not wanting to find out.

Now I open them again.

I'm always the last to walk out of Cissie's bathroom. Today, since the pedal on her flapper bin's broken, I leave a string of dental floss floating inside the toilet bowl. I find Ruan watching her from the other end of the kitchen, lighting up incense sticks and placing them flat on the kitchen counter. He's trying to cover up the smell of glue wafting from the oven.

Most of the walls are stained here, by the way, and the floors are cracked, too. This isn't Cissie's doing, only the nature of her building. It's what makes it affordable for her to rent a flat in this area. Once, when I was sitting on my own on her couch, sober but I guess still half-asleep, I'd tried to count the cracks I could find in her floor-boards. They reminded me then of Sis' Funeka's smile in the days before we'd buried her, and, in a way, I guess they still do. My aunt refused to look at me after Luthando was gone, and though I never attended her funeral, I was told she mistook me for him on her hospital bed. I thought I was lucky, back then, to have escaped the insight of her dementia. Maybe she would've pointed me out as the one who'd killed him.

Instead, I'm here.

Hung over in Newlands, six foot two, bone-thin, soaked through and dripping pipe-rusted water all over Cissie's threshold. In the kitchen, Cissie has the only dry towel in the flat wrapped around her waist. I look in from the door. Then cough loud enough to annoy her.

Really, I say, Cecelia, tell me this isn't typical.

Standing by the stove, Cissie doesn't answer me. Instead, she starts laughing. Or she scoffs, rather. Which is what Cecelia does these days. She scoffs. ·

I watch her take her time as she turns around, and when she's done with that, with giving me and Ruan her performance, she throws me a tattered dishcloth to dry myself off with. Even though it's stupid of me to catch it, that's what I do, and before I can say anything in protest, she tells me to look at what she's busy doing. I look up and Cecelia waves at me.

Dude, she says, can't you see I'm being a breadwinner here? I'm the only one who pays the rent on time on the fourth floor of this damn building. Can't you see that?

In response, I sigh. Then, since she's right, I nod.

I dry my neck and behind my ears. In the bathroom again, I pull on a pair of shorts and find a dry shirt in the hamper. It belongs to her, but it used to be mine, so I put it on. I pat my hair with the dishcloth and hang it on the shower rail to dry. Then I walk around her and open the kitchen windows for air. I'm sure we all need that by now.

I unbolt each latch on the front door and step out onto the balcony. Leaning back against the railing, I breathe out and watch Cissie wiping her brow with a sigh. She gathers the brown goo in the pot with a small wooden spoon and lets it drip slowly into the pit of a yellow bowl. I stand there and she stands there. We stare at each other for a while.

I guess this is how everything moves today. It's like riding on the back of a large, dying mammal. It matches the tepid warmth, and I close my eyes against it. I try not to think about Bhut' Vuyo's message. I try not to think about everything I've had to put away about Luthando, my dead brother, in the days that have grown out into years between us. Instead, I think about how it's the weekend, again. It's the weekend, and this is what the three of us do on days like today.

Sitting cross-legged in the living room, Ruan opens his laptop and starts up the printer on Cissie's coffee table. He feeds paper into the machine and watches as the computer boots up with its usual noise. I suppose you could call this our operation, our way of making a little extra in this place, here in Cape Town, where we are.

To understand it better, you'd have to meet Cecelia.

Cissie's our resident chemist here at West Ridge. She's in charge of cooking the glue we use to hang up our posters; and in order to make it the way Cissie does, you need flour, brown sugar and a small amount of vinegar. You need to pour these into a bowl, add a cup of water and mix thoroughly, making sure to squash out all the lumps from the flour. Have the oven preheated at 180°, bring the bowl to a boil, keep stirring and build up the texture. During this entire process, what helps is to be as patient and attentive as Cecelia when she's cooking a batch. Failing that, you can at least try to be halfway as demanding as she is, and halfway for Cissie, of course, means all the way for the rest of us.

I remember how I'd been out of a job for seven months, once. I was living off the last of my severance pay when Cecelia, who'd just showered and burnt her hand on her new but broken sandwich grill, came to sit next to me on her bed and asked me if I ever considered what would really happen to me the moment I died. That's how things were back then, about two years ago, and I suppose they aren't that different now. It was a warm night in October. The South-Easter had descended on Cape Town to dry-clean our skins, and Cecelia, with her hair dripping and the smell of Pick n Pay conditioner fuming off her scalp, left dark spots of moisture scattered across my *Jobmail* paper.

I told her then how I never thought about that, how thoughts like that wouldn't have allowed me to do what I had done.

Cissie listened with her head tilted, and took a long time before she answered me and said okay. Then she leaned into my chest and closed her eyes to fall asleep, and with everything silent and her flat feeling like an old tomb around us, I bent down to touch her on the part of her finger that was dying. With her eyes still closed, Cissie raised her hand and stuck the burnt finger inside my mouth, and sliding it slowly over my tongue, told me to suck on the skin until it came back to life.

So I did that.

I didn't mind doing it, either.

I watch her now as she opens and closes the oven door. Cissie removes another stray braid from her face and, cupping her left palm, waves away a wisp of smoke. One of the biggest problems she has with me, she says, is that I never pay enough attention to people. Every time I offer someone a shoulder to cry on, Cissie says, my biggest concern is the snot left drying on my shirt. I've told her how I think that's good, how she's phrased that.

I remember the first time she brought it up. It had just started raining outside, and she'd got up half-naked from the mattress we three sometimes shared. It was close to midnight and the room had cloaked itself in complete darkness. I waited a while, then joined her on the wooden floor. I guess neither of us was in a rush to get up again. We took our time, sitting in silence, and the first gray light fingered its way through the slits between her blinds.

Then, before getting up to shower, I guess having proved her point through silence, Cissie said I check the time a lot when people tell me their problems. In response, I told her I'd work on it. Then I looked at my wristwatch.

I guess I'm still working on it.

Even so, while I fail to live up to Cissie's standards for human sympathy, I have a friend who's even worse off than I am. His name is Ruan, and he loses no sleep over that sort of thing. I know this because I've asked him about it.

I mean really. You should hear Ruan speak.

He's our resident printer here at West Ridge. To print out as much ink as he does, you need to buy a regular 60XL cartridge, then take it home and print until it reaches half its capacity. Then steam it open and loosen the blade above the chemical toner. Report this as a defect to the manufacturer, add an image for evidence, and print out their response to take back to the shop for a new pack. Most ink companies will corroborate your story like this by accident. Corporations lose nothing in providing customer care to a single claim from a foreign client. What helps, of course, is to know how to lie as often and as easily as Ruan does.

I watch him lean his head back on Cissie's couch. He has a five-o'clock shadow that runs down half the length of his throat, and his Adam's apple bobs up and down as the printer chugs, pulling in reams of paper ready for all the ink he's defrauded from Cape Town's shop assistants.

This makes us up as a total. You count these two and add me. We make up a team of three, and these days, if you want to know what passes for my social life, just take a look at them, at Ruan and Cecelia.

I know I haven't said much about Ruan yet. For years now, and maybe even before that, Ruan and I have considered ourselves the closest thing we might ever get to kin. I guess that's worked out for me in the end, and maybe for him, too, whenever it needs to. Getting to know him, what you learn first is never to believe anything he says, and what you learn second is that whenever he's high, he'll tell you that his first near-death experience was a download.

I'm not making that up.

Meet him and he's probably coming down or high. The three of us don't manage to stay in between for too long. Ruan will tell you that since he started feeding his plants with the new fertilizer he ordered online, the pigeons have been coming to his flat more than ever. If you listen to him, he'll tell you how these birds travel all the way down from the Philippines and stop over at Maine before they circle back to his windowsill in Sea Point. When I first started to know him, Ruan and I spent a lot of time talking about these birds. He told me he was an asthmatic and introverted child, and that what he knew about bird migrations wasn't from taking a lot of trips to the museum. He told me and Cissie how much these birds meant to him, and even though we didn't understand, we believed him.

Then lastly, there's me.

In case you've been wondering, I was also given a name. My parents got mine from a girl. My mother had a friend who almost went blind from working in a clothing factory in the seventies. They'd both been students at Lovedale College before my mother moved on to Fort Hare, and when they reunited again, years later, under the dome of an East London factory shop, the friend was mending clothes to put her daughter Lindanathi through school. I suppose that child, listless in a corner, wearing knee-length socks and wielding a bag full of textbooks, became a sign of hope for my mother. She convinced my father to give me the same name.

Lindanathi means "wait with us." What I'm meant to be waiting for, or who I'm meant to be waiting with, I was never told.

It's just what my name is.

I'm Nathi, and of the three of us, I'm the one who's supposed to be dying. In order to do as much standing around as I do, you need to be one of the forty million human beings currently infected with the immunodeficiency virus. Then you need to stand at your friend's computer and design a poster over his shoulder, one telling these people you're here to help them. Then you need to provide them with your details—tell them you prefer email or SMS—and then start selling them your pills.

What helps, of course, is to try to forget about it as much as possible. Which is what I do.

Maybe it's this whole slavery thing, Cissie says.

Leaning on her balcony, I try to press reply on my cellphone, but my fingers pause over the buttons. They feel like paper straws. I stare at the blinking cursor.

In the kitchen, Cissie stirs another ladle of water into the glue. This morning, her braids are rolled up in a neat ball at the top of her head, a new style the three of us have started to favor more and more for her. When she moves, a few of the strands loosen and fall like tassels across her chest, and she flicks them away from the stove in a single shake with her shoulders. Cissie has a way of making the smallest things obey her, and I guess that includes me and Ruan.

I put my cellphone away. These days, she's always wearing a different pack of synthetic hair on her head. Sometimes the color she chooses is black, at other times it's a blue shade, and at other times it's this color I can't even describe to you—like silver or aqua or teal or something. Ruan and I have seen her in the red and blonde ones a lot. Cissie wears them on her head all day and all of them, she says, are more flammable than a wick dipped in paraffin. She tells us to think of her as a human match, with a dormant fire ready to burst into flame between her brains, which is a nice way of telling people not to fuck with you. Or at least the nicest way I've heard.

I can feel my cellphone's weight against my thigh. Leaning back on the railing, I push out three slow breaths for composure. Out on the balcony, the weather changes faces. Spring is stalling, still a month away, but the sun's rays warm up my skin like geyser water. They throw dappled light across the empty corridor.

Ruan and I have been squatting here for the past few nights, somewhere between falling asleep and overdosing on Cissie's couch. Cissie's building, this unattractive cream-colored six-story called West Ridge Heights, was converted from an old ground-level nursing home in the late eighties. It sits tucked away in Newlands, a docile suburb, just a few streets off the main road, and it's one of the two holes Ruan and I have chosen to call our homes, this year. Or maybe just for the winter, if you want to take Ruan's view of things.

In any case, this is where Cissie cooks her glue for us. You take a look and the building has the usual overgrown grass, the usual stained ceilings, and the usual dirty lino in its single-lift lobby. There's a tile missing here and there, with a broken full-length mirror and plastic potted plants leaning back in most of its corners. There isn't much security to speak of, and below, on the ground floor, there's a young girl who plays by herself in a small courtyard, building cities with loose pieces of concrete from the broken water fountain. I always wave at her when Ruan and I come over to crash. Often, she just looks up and stares at me with vacant eyes. Then she runs back under the awning and disappears into places I can't imagine from up here on the fourth. In between these encounters, I've learned her name is Ethelia.

Inside, I hear Cissie talking again.

I'm being serious, she says. Look, just think about this thing for a moment.

I try to.

I mean, it's pretty much a habit for us, by now. What we're doing is having one of our talks about what to do for Last Life. Last Life is the name we've come up with for what happens to me during my last year on the planet. Like always, we stayed up for most of the previous night with the question. We finished the wine first. Then we moved on to the bottle of benzene.

Ruan looks up and says, dude, explain this slavery thing to me. He gets up to take a thin book from the counter and flops himself down on a torn bean-bag. Then he starts reading the book—*A Happy Death* by Camus—from the back, his eyes training the sentences inward, as if the French author had written a Japanese manga.

Cissie just says her word again.

Slavery.

She raises her hand and waves the gooey ladle in a small circle above the bowl.

You know what I mean, she says. The three of us, we're basically slaves.

From my side, I remain quiet. I just watch them like I sometimes do. I mean honestly. It's Ruan who usually brings us all this pathos.

The three of us aren't slaves. Ruan, Cissie and I each wrote matric in the country's first batch of Model C's. In common, our childhoods had the boomerangs we used to throw with the neighborhood kids, the rollerblades and the green buckets of space goo. The Sticky Hands with their luminous jelly fingers, each digit rumored to be toxic, which we clotted with wet earth on the first day back from the store and threw into our green pools for cleansing. The Grow Monsters which we watched expanding inside our toilet bowls with awe, and the tracks we dug for our Micro Machines before the day ended, when the orange light would come down and tint the neighborhood roof tiles the color of a lightbulb filament.

Ease. Everything my little brother Luthando never got to have.

For all that time, I remember LT topless in denim shorts and wearing a thin silver chain. Luthando played marbles, that's what he knew most of all to do with his hands. My brother wasn't tough, but he fancied himself a township *ou*. I remember how he didn't know what a spinning top was before I gave him mine. We used the laces from his Chuck Taylors to spin it, and later that night, I was quiet when he refused to drink the water my mother poured for us at the dinner table, telling me later that he'd wanted to preserve the taste of beef in his mouth.

Inside the kitchen, Cissie tries to drive home her point. What if babies cry because birth is the first form of human incarceration? What if it's a lasting shock to the consciousness to be imprisoned inside the human body? If the flesh is something that's meant to go off from the beginning, doesn't that make it an ill fit, since the consciousness, naturally amorphous, is antithetical to disintegration?

Still stirring the glue in her yellow bowl, Cissie asks if we understand.

I can't really tell.

I don't think LT is still around. Maybe it's because my body's breaking down that she's speaking to us like this, or maybe it's because her own body's fading away from her. You can't always tell with Cecelia. It could be everyone's body that's bothering her.

I walk back inside, anyway, and take the spoon from her. She gives me a mock head-butt with her match head, and then she sits on the counter to light up a cigarette. Sighing with relief, she closes her eyes to suck in the carcinogens.

From behind his book, Ruan tells us we aren't selling enough pills. He places the book aside and looks up at me. Of course, this isn't really news to us.

I tell him that my case manager said she'd give me a call. For months now, I say, my insurers, I think they've been holding out on me.

Ruan sits up.

Jesus, Nathi, he says, don't tell me they've started reviewing your case. He pulls his computer onto his lap. Quick, dude, he says, *gooi* me her name and email.

This is Ruan's solution for most of our problems. Mention something to him and he'll ask you for a name and an email address. Right now, I shrug, since I don't have either one.

I guess I could find out, I say.

I keep stirring.

I tell myself this is what's important.

I wipe my brow like I've been watching Cissie do all morning. When I look up, I find her closing her eyes, leaning back on the kitchen counter. She blows out a pair of smoke rings. Then her hand drops to ash the last of her cigarette, and she says it again, this word she's been using on us all morning.

Slavery.

On the bean-bag, Ruan doesn't respond. He goes back to reading and I take out my cellphone. I plug it into the charger next to the stove, and, using my other hand to stir, I read the text message from my uncle.

Lindanathi, my uncle Bhut' Vuyo says, *ukhulile ngoku*, you've come of age.

He tells me I haven't been seen in too long. I read this second line for a while before I delete the message.

Returning to the glue, the relief I expect to wash over me doesn't arrive. Instead, I think of each word I've read off the screen. I think of coming of age in the way Bhut' Vuyo means. Then I think of my last night in Du Noon, and about those two words, *ukhulile ngoku*, and of coming of age once more.

My case manager calls my cellphone close to an hour later. We've put away Cissie's cooked glue in plastic containers to cool off in the freezer, and we've taken up our noses what's left of the tube of industrial-strength glue she keeps in her drawer. It's now just a little after one, and we're sprawled sideways across Cissie's living-room floor, our lungs full of warmth from n-hexane. When I don't pick up and answer my case manager's call, my cellphone seems to melt inside my palm. It's a strange sensation, but one you get used to after a while.

With another hour passing, we watch as Ruan pulls his baseball cap over his forehead. He plays "By This River" by Brian Eno on his laptop, tapping the repeat button under the seek bar, and then the next hour arrives and Cissie hands us three Ibuprofens each. She pops them out of a new 500-milligram bubble pack, and we take them with glasses of milk and clumps of brown sugar. From where I'm sitting, I can still feel the warmth from the glue expanding through me, a thick liquid spilling out from my chest and kneading into my fingertips. The sunlight casts a wide flat beam over the coffee table, and after we've swallowed, we place the tumblers holding the rest of our milk between its narrow legs. I close my eyes again and hear my cellphone calling out for me. Its vibration feels like a small hand running over my thigh, and when I pick it up, my heart squeezes into itself as I think of Bhut' Vuyo. I see Luthando's stepfather stretching his vest under his heavy blue overalls, sitting inside a sweating phone container and hefting a fistful of change, but then I look down and the code reads 011, connecting my line to the grid in Joburg.

I place the receiver back against my ear, hearing the sound of a hundred telephones ringing in unison, and then the sound of my case manager climbing up from underneath this din, shouting at me through a deep ocean of static. The missing copper—I imagine kilometers of it stolen from our skyline each year—leaves a yawning gap of silence between our sentences, and then a big wind pushes behind her voice when she tells me about missing another meeting, how it means my insurance will have no choice but to cut me off. She tells me they haven't received a sheet with my CD4 count for close to five months now, and that I should know better than to be this reckless with their program.

I'm sitting down as I listen to this. Since I can't do anything else, I nod at the table.

Something that's not difficult to figure out about me and my case manager is that we've never gotten along. Not in any real sense of the word. I only know her as Sis' Thobeka, never having bothered to ask her for a full name, and in my head, she's just one of the many medical bureaucrats I'll have to pass through on my way out. She calls me from an air-conditioned office in Joburg, and there isn't much else to say about us. Except maybe this one time, when she took up my case about four years ago. She told me that she'd fallen into her line of work owing to a compulsion she had to assist the frail. She'd grown tired of her nursing job at Baragwanath, however, of all the men, women and children that got swept into the intensive care unit on her watch, most of them broken into soft and wet pieces.

This introduction left a reluctant mark on me. On occasion, I still think of her as existing between then and now, and of the number of people she had to witness turning into powder. Maybe this makes it easier for me to stomach her: that she has this knowledge of loss beneath the protocol. I even told her, once, how I'd got my virus by accident. I remember her silence that day. The two of us stayed on the line for a while, and in the end, she only said: okay. Then she coughed and we carried on. To this day, I doubt she thinks it prudent to believe anything I say. Not that I'd want that from her. This suits the two of us just fine.

On the line now, I tell her, okay.

Okay what?

I've got a meeting scheduled.

You have a meeting scheduled, she says. When is this?

It's today.

Well, that's good then, Lindanathi. Take yourself to that meeting today, and then fax us a proof of attendance with your CD4 count sheet. We've approved the latest shipment of your medications, but now you have to do your part for us and make the program work. Do you understand?

I do. I tell her that.

You have a good care package here, she tells me. Don't let it go to waste over foolishness.

I won't.

Right.

I tell her again that I won't.

Look, it's in your hands, isn't it?

It is.

Well then, she says. We've added benefits for you Silver members. We could move you up in a few months' time if you fixed up your file. We've had to scale back on the Platinum option, though, so I would suggest a Gold membership for now.

I nod. I can hear Sis' Thobeka pecking on her keyboard as I consider the options. Voices murmur in her office, and I begin to drift off as she details the premiums.

She lets a minute pass in silence before she asks me if I'm doing fine in any case, if I'm okay despite everything else that's the matter with me.

I blink, and I'm about to answer her when she says she has another call coming in. I wait for her when she tells me to wait, and I'm still doing that when her voice turns into a dial tone.

Later, when I open my eyes, I find Ruan and Cissie staring down at me. Their brows crease as they edge towards my place on the floor, their outlines melting into the walls stained and cracked behind them.

Cissie says, Nathi, are you okay?

My mouth feels blow-dried, packed thick with stiff clouds of cotton wool.

I look up and ask them the same. I say, are you okay?

In response, Cissie points a finger at her ear. Then she gets on her knees, takes my hand, and says, Nathi, your phone's dead.

The way I got to know them, by the way, my two closest friends here, is that we met at one of the new HIV and drug-counseling sessions cropping up all over the city. We were in the basement parking lot of the free clinic in Wynberg. The seminar room upstairs had been locked up and taped shut, there'd been a mercury spill, and our group couldn't meet in there on account of the vapors being toxic to human tissue. Instead, they arranged us in the basement parking lot, and in two weeks we got used to not being sent upstairs for meetings. I did, in any case, and that was enough for me in the beginning.

In those days, I attended the meetings alone. I'd catch a taxi from Obs over to Wynberg for an afternoon's worth of counseling. By the end of my first month, when the seminar room had been swept once, and then twice, and then three times by a short man who wore a blue contamination meter over his chest, each time checking out clean, everyone decided they preferred it down below, and so that's where we stayed.

Maybe we all want to be buried here, I said.

It had been the first time I'd spoken in group. Talking always took me a while, back then, but the remark succeeded in making a few of them laugh. It won me chuckles even from the old-timers, and later, I wrote down my first addiction story to share with the group. It was from a film I saw adapted from a book I wasn't likely to read. Ruan and Cissie arrived on the following Wednesday.

I noticed them immediately. Something seemed to draw us in from our first meeting. In the parking lot, we eyeballed each other for a while before we spoke. During the coffee break, we stood by the serving table in front of a peeling Toyota *bakkie*, mumbling tentatively towards each other's profiles. I learned that Cecelia was a teacher. She pulled week-long shifts at a day-care center just off Bridge Street in Mowbray, and she was there on account of the school's accepting its first openly positive pupil. Ruan, who was leaning against the plastic table, gulping more than sipping at the coffee in his paper cup, said that he suffocated through his life by working on the top floor of his uncle's computer firm. He was there to shop for a social issue they could use for their corporate responsibility strategy. He called it CRS, and Cissie and I had to ask him what he meant.

In the end, I guess I was impressed. I told them how I used to be a lab assistant at Peninsula Tech, and how in a way this was part of how I'd got to be sick with what I have.

When we sat back down again, we listened to the rest of the members assess each other's nightmares. They passed them around with a familiar casualness. Mark knew about Ronelle's school fees, for instance, and she knew about Linette's hepatitis, and all of us knew that Linda had developed a spate of genital warts over September. She called them water warts, when she first told us, and, like most of her symptoms, she blamed them on the rain.

That day, when the discussion turned to drug abuse, as it always did during the last half-hour of our sessions, the three of us had nothing to add. I looked over at Ruan and caught him stashing a grin behind his fist, while on my other side, Cecelia blinked up at the ceiling. I didn't need any more evidence for our kinship.

The meeting lasted the full two hours, and when it came to an end, I collected my proof of attendance and exchanged numbers with Ruan and Cecelia. I suppose we said our goodbyes at the entrance of the parking lot that day, and later, within that same week I think, we were huffing paint thinner together in my flat in Obs.

Coming down from Industrial isn't as easy as pulling in your first huff. It isn't for me, and I guess it never is for my two friends, either. I've put the cellphone back on the charger after Sis' Thobeka's call and the three of us are taking turns splashing our faces with cold water from the kitchen tap. When we're done, I remove my phone from the socket by the stove. Then Cissie bolts her door and we take the lift down to the ground floor.

The atmosphere feels warm and slippery on my skin, and my mind instructs me to glide, so I push my arms out and try to do that. I slide my fingers across the walls as we walk through the mouth of the lobby, balancing with my hands and trying not to slip, feeling as if the plastic tiles are peeling beneath my feet.

We follow Cissie across the grassy oval. Ethelia, the little girl who builds and restores peace to concrete empires, has disappeared. Her cities lie in ruin, scattered in a loose ring around the water fountain.

Cissie leads the way past the reception desk; Ruan and I take our time making it out of the front entrance. I put my one foot after the other, and begin to feel my breath heating up like a bed of coals. When I cough, it's a noise that goes on for a while, rattling inside the numbness in my chest, but it doesn't do much to clear it.

I take out my cellphone. I've decided to deposit money into Bhut' Vuyo's account. I ask him for his account number, but the message won't send. It displays a red x, meaning I'm out of airtime.

We tumble forward again. Cissie buzzes the parking-lot gate open and we wend a curving path through Newlands's leafy streets. We head down towards the main road, where we stand for a few minutes, smoking cigarettes under a bus awning and leaning our heads against a bright McDonald's ad, balancing each other as we wait for a taxi. Ruan and Cissie keep blurring together in the small space in front of me. To pass the time, Ruan starts telling us a joke he's lost the punch line to. We wait another two minutes before catching a taxi headed out to Wynberg.

Through the taxi window, the sky appears heavy, having grown overcast. The light bounces off the surface like a silver coin, a spill of mercury. When we pierce through Claremont's invisible epidermis, I look down at my hands and find no blood beneath my fingernails. We slow down for an Engen garage and I raise my head again, not sure why I searched through my fingers a moment ago. The thought comes to me that Bhut' Vuyo might still take offense to my money, whether or not I deem it clean enough for him.

For a moment, I think about that, the idea of my money. The three of us remain afloat on what's left of the n-hexane in our blood, sitting one next to the other, two rows from the empty back seat.

The driver pulls over at the garage, and I lean forward and feel something jam inside my head. Small orange shapes burst inside the taxi, and from behind my eyelids, I envision myself laughing with Cissie and Ruan, the three of us wearing tailored suits and acting jubilantly, our fingers rolling joints from tall heaps of two-hundred-rand notes.

These days, when we run out of tubes of Industrial, Ruan and I take solace in each other's misery on Earth, the two of us comparing comedowns as we wait for Cissie to finish her shift. We reload airtime and detail the planet's shortcomings, never disappointing each other with news of well-being or fortune.

When we first started using, though, Ruan and I would sometimes go on runs together for Industrial. They used to offload the boxes in Epping, back then, and then transport the surplus to Bellville, where they mixed the tubes for distribution. I'd call him about a deal, and I'd say, Ruan, tell me what you think about this one. We mostly stayed in the south whenever we had enough money to buy a tube, where the cut of the glue wasn't always guaranteed to come out potent. Still, I remember this one day, when I got a lead on a wholesaler in the north. He was a new dealer, an out-of-towner who'd taken a room at the Little House in Belhar.

When I phoned him, Ruan took a while to pick up. Then I heard him shifting his weight. I had to wait for him to finish drumming a stream of urine into the bowl.

Nooit, my friend, he said when he was done.

I heard him hanging over the basin, pushing a dispenser for soap, opening a tap.

Dude, I said, you haven't even thought about this.

I don't have to, he said.

I paused. Well, it's the best lead we've had. I don't want to brag about it.

He was quiet.

I tried him again. You seriously haven't heard a thing about it? Not a thing.

He could be an asshole sometimes.

Maybe it's fresh, I said.

It might be fresh, he said. He agreed to that much, at least.

Listen, he said.

I listened. I heard him kick a door open, walk a short distance and settle himself in a booth. He was drinking a milkshake, I could tell. I sighed. It meant Ruan had gone through a tube of glue alone on his living-room floor, and now he was sitting up the street from his flat at The Blue China, an ice-cream bar we sometimes lumbered into after getting high. The milkshake would no doubt be a banana mint with chocolate shavings and a light sprinkle of cinnamon. I knew it well because it's the only thing we ever ordered.

This guy has money, I said to him, still thinking it over.

Money, Ruan said.

He wanted me to hear his boredom. It was a hint to get me off the line. I heard him pull in a suck from his shake, which meant he'd already scooped the toppings off the foam with a teaspoon, and that he'd set the teaspoon on a saucer over his doubled napkin. It was a tic. Cissie and I sometimes teased him about it. We said he'd keep this up for as long as his hands were hung on the ends of his wrists, or at least until all our motor functions gave in from the glue.

Your hands are weird, I said to him, giving up.

Really?

Yes.

Really, they are. Ruan has these long thin fingers that shoot out of pale, crusted knuckles. The skin on them looks thin, almost translucent, and his palms sweat out ten liters a day.

It's like you were something else before a person, I said.

He laughed. Dude, that's offside.

Let's go north, then.

Ruan laughed again. Have you talked to Cissie?

No.

You should.

Why?

I already knew why. It was a good reason, too: I didn't think it was safe enough for her. This was before the Little House on the Prairie, an old *tik* den based in the south of Bellville, would get on the news, but we all knew Belhar deserved its reputation back then. Even before Mr. Big had taken over the plot on Modderdam Road, there was the story of the guy who'd walked out of the door without his hands on him, the stumps on his arms wetting the cuffs on his pants. I pressed a button and got Ruan louder on the line.

Why should I? I asked him again.

I don't know, he said, but the damned should stick together, don't you think?

I don't disagree with you, I said.

We pull out of the garage. The *gaartjie* hangs his waist out of the window, his long tongue chafing against his cracked lips, his large voice calling out for Wynberg. He's a young guy, tattooed and thin, weathered, like most of the *gaartjies* who work in the south. The glass edge eats into his stomach as we speed past Cavendish, his gold chain rattling around his neck like a piece of snapped film on a reel. This is what you do when you cast your net for the strays, his body seems to say. You push yourself out into their air and echo.

I breathe and look ahead. Ruan and Cissie tap their cell-phones as our driver stops again. He scoops up another harried passenger—a woman of around sixty, wearing navy slacks and a dirty cashmere sweater—and then we stay quiet for the rest of the trip. I lean back and feel my neck, moist and cold, pressing hard against the taxi's torn plastic seating.

We score a lot of our customers at group meetings for the HI Virus here in Cape Town. We've been to meetings as far out as Hout Bay, too, to Khayelitsha, Langa and Bellville. We've been to two or three in Paarl, and once, when we hitched the twelve o'clock train from Rondebosch, we went out to Simon's Town. It's part of it, to get around the way we do. We hand out pamphlets to anyone who wants to place an order. Most of our clients don't make enough to meet the criteria needed for cover-age: they come to us for a pack, or just enough to taper off an initial treatment. I like to imagine it depending on the stage of their illness, but most of it comes down to what they have in their pockets.

The taxi drops us off in Wynberg. I start looking around for a place to buy airtime, but then I realize I have no change to pay the hawkers with. My eyes drop to the thighs of the women vendors, and I begin to feel embarrassed, running my gaze over the wares on their tables. For the first time, I notice how they look like a jury, seated on a row of cracked SAB crates. The old women squint at the world through the leather of their dark, folded faces, their eyes glassy with glaucoma, each orb like a marble spinning in wet earth. Globules of sweat draw runnels down their temples, and their pulses beat together like the hearts of small mammals. Maybe they've heard from Bhut' Vuyo. In front of their hunger, I pull out more lint from the recesses of my pockets. Then Cissie pulls me away.

The three of us knit our way through the stream of daytime traffic. In the sky above, the day's gone full gray, but still holds on to an ember of its heat. Ruan and Cissie don't say much. We share another cigarette as we weave through the shoppers, hawkers and *gaartjies*. Then we turn down a one-way that leads us to the clinic.

The clinic is this white building with a low green fence and a face-brick finish. Ruan and Cissie walk around the boom gate and I follow a step behind. We make our way down to the basement, where they've added extra light fixtures to the ceiling. It surprises me, to see how much brighter the place looks. They've painted the walls, and my vision takes a moment to adjust.

We take our seats on plastic chairs set up in a circle in the middle of the space, waiting for the session to begin. Mary, our red-haired counselor, sits on a plastic chair opposite the three of us, a halo from the fluorescents sketching a delicate crown around her Technicolor bob.

I close my eyes for a while.

Sitting in group, everything bears a trace of what you've seen before. I remember how once, when we were ten years old, my brother and I visited my grand-aunt in King William's Town. It was summer, and one Saturday morning we stole out to Candies and Novelties, a small store hidden behind the town's post office. We were looking for firecrackers. For most of that summer, my brother and I had scoured the town to find thick black widows we could stuff into Cherry Coke cans. We had a plan to set them up as booby traps for the town pigeons.

Inside the store, we spent some time in front of the shop counter, smudging it with fingerprints as we ogled the TV-game cartridges on display. Then we went up and down the aisles, drinking in all the toys we could never afford.

Luthando and I took two different aisles at a time, heading out in opposite directions, and it wasn't long before a woman who looked like Mary called out to us. She had Mary's skin and hair. When she demanded to know what we wanted, we told her we were just browsing, and she said we could do that from outside.

I was used to it and said nothing, but after we left, Luthando wanted to go back inside and spit on her forehead. It was pale and as large as a bed sheet, he told me, and I laughed, but I stopped him. I'd been warned by my mother. We were to act like visitors in my grand-aunt's town.

Cissie touches my knee and shakes me awake. When I open my eyes, I find Neil talking to his feet. My mouth feels scorched and my hands are damp. I crane my neck to take a better look at him.

With Neil, I guess there isn't much to say. He's a former math teacher from a gated estate in Westlake. He's been divorced twice and has rails on both of his arms, the result of a heroin habit that followed from years of blow. He taught private school for thirteen years, he says, and maybe that's the reason no one likes him here. I've heard some of the older members say he won't make it through the year, and if you look at him, that isn't hard to believe. This comes from the old users, mostly. Guys from a clinic in Diep River, and one from Strand. They look at him and shake their heads.

Today, Neil's dressed in a short-sleeved flannel shirt tucked into a pair of pressed chinos. He's a thin guy, with a gnawed coat-hanger for a frame, and his hair is dark and matted, hanging low enough to touch his shoulders. He's wearing a crucifix around his neck, and above it a pair of broad-framed glasses, each lens flashing under the basement's new fluorescent lights.

Like most addicts, Neil has an excuse for each time he feels his life cracking open. Today, he wants a mass deportation of all the illegal immigrants in Cape Town. We should start off with the Nigerians, he tells us, and follow it up with the Somalis.

I look over and find Cissie rolling her eyes.

Out of the three of us, Cissie's the one Neil bores the most. I remember how she once asked us why he didn't just get HIV already. Maybe it was an awful thing to say, but Ruan and I laughed because it was true. Even though Neil's a serf in his community, he's a nobleman in ours. We could've pulled a lot of money out of him.

Neil has these long, bony hands that flop around him when he speaks, and today, he has one of them girded in a bright spotted bandage. He waves it and tells us he cut himself with a *lolly*—an old glass pipe he's never changed since buying his first straw—and that he passed out on his kitchen floor. Raising his other hand, he tells us he's managed to keep away from the ice this week.

Then Mary thanks him and the rest of us nod.

I guess this isn't really dramatic.

If anything, Neil's brought our drug talk forward by an hour and a half, and when Olive stands up to speak next, it seems this trend might persist for the rest of our session.

Olive suffers from an undiagnosed respiratory obstruction, and on occasion it clogs the walls of her larynx, causing her breath to make a racket on its way out. I can hear the air pushing out from her throat, a wheeze that reaches me from six members away. Maybe it's a song, a whistle of the damage she carries inside her, or maybe it's just human wear: the kind we all have, waiting to waylay us.

Like most places filled with the sick and the dying, there's always an opportunity to learn something about being a person here. Our parking lot turns into an academy at times, and we get educated on the survival of people like Leonardo and people like Linette, on people like Neil and people like Olive. Maybe it's best for me to forget my own troubles and grow a greater sympathy for others. Like Cecelia, this could be what Bhut' Vuyo wants from me.

During my time here, I've learned everything there is to know about Olive. Her last name is De Villiers, and she was born to pious Presbyterians, a young couple rooted in a community church in Maitland. Her family clipped its extensions to preserve its piety, and as an only child, Olive grew up with an urgent need to see other people. Her teenage years were split between Hanover and Grassy Park, and she says she watched her friends breathing out thick white plumes for years before she joined them at sixteen. She's a single mother now, headed towards the end of her thirties, and she has the kind of hard but pleasant face you often see in women from the Flats. She works as a soup-kitchen cook at a backyard orphanage in Lavender Hill, and when she stands up to talk, every story she tells us circles the same subject. It's about her struggle to form a relationship with Emile, her son and only child.

He's just a child, she says. I know, I know, but he's starting to make out that everything I do is a *gemors*. I can *sommer* hear it in the way the child speaks to me when I visit my parents and they have people over.

Olive's dressed in black today. She has on a ribbed polo-neck sweater and a sea-colored *doek* that holds her dreadlocks in a neat parting. Her hair's pushed back into two thick columns that fall away in rolling curves behind her ears, and her dreadlocks are tinted a color that, depending on the kind of day you're having, reminds you of either sunset or rust.

Today, I can't help it.

I fill up with an image of bursting pipes.

Inside my pocket, I release my cellphone. Then I knead my knuckles and crack them. I decide to circle my thoughts around Olive.

The worst day she ever had as a user, she's told us, began

when she forgot her son's name. She tried to ask him for it, putting on a wide smile to throw him off guard, but she could tell he knew. Olive couldn't recall the three years in which she'd met Emile's father, in which Emile had been conceived, and in which she'd given birth to him. It had all disappeared, she said, and she'd had to watch her son growing up without her smell, knowing only the instruction of his grandparents.

Today, she shares her latest suspicions about Emile. Olive says her apologies have started to harden him, to make him believe she's a woman who deserves nothing better than scorn. Listening to her, the rest of us nod.

Olive's the one I've come to feel for the most in our meetings, but there's nothing I can do to help. She suffers from something I have no treatment for, and I can only watch her when she drops her head in shame. Often, I've had to avert my eyes when Olive starts to weep, but today my gaze remains passive and arrested on her frame. I realize that my feelings for her have been drained from me, and that I can no longer use her as a hiding place. The two of us sit apart, returned to the distance we once knew as strangers: two people walking into a basement parking-lot in the daytime, heads bowed and smiles coated with nicotine.

In most meetings, half the members don't make the move to draw close to one another. We enter each session prepared to deflect the counsel leader, whose job is to put whatever remains of us under glass. If you listen to counselors, they'll tell you they want full disclosure in meetings, but most of us know to hand the facts out in small doses only. Therapy won't walk you home after you pack up the chairs. Telling too much about yourself can leave you feeling broken into, as if your head were a conquered city offered to the circle for pillaging. This is how we know Olive won't finish Emile's story in front of us. I close my eyes again.

One week after I deregistered from university and my mother

grew resolute in her decision to bar me from her home, I began to visit prostitutes in Mowbray, a block up from the bridge in Rosebank. I never slept with any of them, but one morning, returning late from having gone out for happy hour at a bar on lower Long, and after allowing another one to fondle my penis through my jeans next to the bath house on Orange Street, I bungled the directions to my flat and asked the taxi driver to pull over at the Engen garage. I wanted to buy a spinach-and-feta pie, a pack of Doritos and a bottle of water. That's when I saw them—across the main road, shivering. When our eyes met, they began to beckon to me all at once.

My first reaction was amusement. Then suddenly I felt wanted, in a way that surprised me with its strength. I walked towards them, crossing over a traffic island, and stood by while they took turns soliciting me for sex. In the end, I gave them the bag of chips and went back to the taxi.

In the weeks that followed, I passed by there often. I made a habit of talking to them, making bribes out of what I bought from the service station, and we'd stand in the cold together. I remember how shattered their faces looked, as if they were the survivors of a protracted battle. Yet I also recall the feeling of comfort they gave me, as if I could disappear in between them.

In the end it was this feeling, its ability to surprise and take hold of me, that redirected me from moroseness when the nights drew to a close, finding me once more on my own, standing in front of my kitchen counter, boiling curry noodles from a plastic packet or decanting leek soup into a saucepan. I suppose they saw that in me, and I located it in them, too, my need. Maybe I've been looking for that same thing in Olive, another woman who's put her battles before me, having ruined herself with straws of bitter crystals.

It always happens, Olive says, and my heart is like this. It's a paper in pieces.

I watch her as she wipes her tears. When Olive sits back

down, a moment passes before the drug trend is broken. I guess this brings a little relief. This part of our talks, the HIV section, is usually when Ruan, Cissie and I start with our orders. We assign one person to take down notes, and whoever's chosen for the duty has to catalog the stage of the disease in each member. You note an infected spouse, distinguishing symptoms and patterns of remission. Then all three of us work out a treatment plan before we sell it to them.

Today, I signal to my friends that I'll volunteer for the job. It might take my thoughts off Bhut' Vuyo. Relieved, Ruan and Cissie nod and lean back in their chairs. Ta Lloyd takes up his turn to speak next.

I don't really know what to say about Ta Lloyd, either. I've heard members say he's the oldest guy in our group, but no one knows that for sure. We've all had trouble believing him. When I first joined here at Wynberg, Linette told me his story was make-believe. Ta Lloyd told them he got sick on the job as a paramedic. This was in the mid-nineties. He says they gave him an emergency van to pay him off. Today, he's seated just two chairs from me. When he gets up, he says there's a man who's giving his wife a cure. I turn around and catch Ruan looking up from his cellphone. Paying the two of us no mind, Ta Lloyd continues with his story.

This cure, he says, it's a reality.

That's the word he uses.

We listen to him like we're supposed to, and on her side of the circle, Mary starts to furrow her brow. In her role as our counsel leader, Mary's duties include making sure all our meetings remain civil and well informed. Sometimes she'll intervene when the misinformation piles too high. In this way, you could say she takes the role of rearranging our history. Playing the part of proofreader, Mary fixes us wherever she finds us mistaken, adding her own revisions to the stories we use to explain ourselves to the world. Today, she chooses to remain quiet, however, and like the rest of us, she waits for Ta Lloyd to finish telling us his part.

I reach into my pocket for my phone. Then I start taking down my notes.

It's strange, I know, he says, but look, I swear to you. This man came to Site C not two months ago. He's a medical doctor.

He pauses for a moment before pointing a finger at Neil.

He's a white man, too, Neil, just like you.

On either side of him, some of the members bow their heads and stifle their laughter. Then Ta Lloyd widens his grin, but the math teacher swats him away.

Jesus, Lloyd, Neil says, would you get on with it?

Our oldest member does.

I guess I thought I saw my father the first time I saw Ta Lloyd. Imagine a squat guy who's just crested his mid-fifties. He has a receding hairline, a salt-and-pepper beard, and he stays in good shape for his age and for the type of place we're in. He's sturdy from what the hospital pays for him to take down his throat each morning, and he drives a Ford Transit with a cracked ceiling, hauling kids to school and back in Site C. His wife, whose positive status they've decided to keep a secret, concealed from both her family and her colleagues, works a till at the Pick n Pay in St George's Mall. She rings up groceries, like I once had to do myself.

Ta Lloyd continues to describe his new doctor. He's opened up a hostel at Site C, he says. It's a place with board and decent facilities.

That's where we've sent Nandipha, he says. That doctor? He told my wife to stop working one week ago. Remember when I told you last month that Nandi had another fainting spell? Well, it happened again.

Ta Lloyd rubs a palm over his mouth, and on my left, Cissie inches her chair forward, and so do Ruan and I. The thing about these fainting spells is that they've come up before. The three of us, exchanging glances like we're doing now? That's from the time I fell on my face from one. We listen as Ta Lloyd explains.

It's not easy, I know, he says. It's not an easy thing to believe. Even in Khayelitsha, not many of us believe.

The rest of us nod.

This doctor, Ta Lloyd says. He told me I shouldn't give Nandi any more ARVs. I swear. He said if I stopped giving Nandipha my pills, he would help us.

I look up and find Mary glowering at him. Like most professionals, she doesn't believe Ta Lloyd should be sharing his prescription with his wife—it's the way most professionals think about the pills. Still, the way Ta Lloyd's story unfolds, the hospital's penance didn't extend to cover his wife's illness. Mary continues to stare at him while he speaks. The rest of us know where this is headed.

I close my eyes and wait for my blood to drum my pulse into my ears, a sound I've always found reassuring. Sometimes, I like to imagine I can hear my illness spinning inside my arteries, that it's rinsing itself and thinning out.

I hear Mary's voice again.

Lloyd, she says, I think that's enough, don't you? We've had our fill.

It doesn't usually take her this long.

I want you to stop this, she says, and listen to me carefully, okay? What we're here for is to lighten each other's burdens, not to spread lies from crackpots. I hope you take Nandipha out of that hostel, too. You're putting your wife at a very big risk with this nonsense.

Her cheeks draw in as she pushes herself up from her chair. It doesn't happen a lot, but it's easy to tell when she's upset.

I mean, if money's the problem here, she says, then why don't you just come upstairs with me after the session? We can easily look up a treatment plan for Nandipha. Of course, she should be present, but time and time again you've refused to bring her to our meetings, haven't you? You think it's good that she hides her status from medical professionals.

Ta Lloyd starts to nod.

For Pete's sake, Mary says, don't just agree with me. You need to stop spreading this nonsense and putting your family in danger. There's no cure for HIV, but as you can see for yourself, it's a condition anyone can live with.

She turns around to confirm this with the rest of us, and we nod, doing our part like we're meant to. When I look over, I find Ta Lloyd doing the same.

Yes, Mary, he says.

Right, that's enough then, she says. You can sit back down now. She starts scanning the room for the next volunteer.

Please remember, the rest of you, she tells us, we're here to help each other heal.

When no one volunteers, Mary starts flipping through the attendance roster, ticking off our names.

Let's have one more speaker, shall we? Then we can break for coffee and biscuits.

Relieved, we do as we're told. Ta Lloyd sits back down and I watch his face going slack from his forehead down to his jaw. When the fluorescents flicker twice over our circle, I look up. Then I wonder about all the other people mending their lives on the floors above us. I remember once seeing a woman there who had what I have, compounded with acute tuberculosis. Her salivary glands had blown out as wide as the cheeks of a Bubble Eye goldfish, and she was there to dispute the window-period of her illness, a complication which had rendered her results indeterminate. When the nurses ignored her complaints, she turned around and laughed at them with such exuberant bitterness, the rest of us couldn't help but look up from our laps. Swiveling on her heel, the woman hurled her objections at the waiting room, next, condemning each of us for our silence.

This is what I think of now as we sit in our circle. Cissie places her hand on my knee again, and when she does it. this time, the table holding our coffee begins to tremble.

I guess I don't know where to lead us next. My uncle is a man set on changing the nature of everything I've known here, and I don't know where to walk to that's flung far enough from his reach. Maybe I should accept this and no longer go on fighting him.

Done with the session, Ruan, Cissie and I decide to go for a pizza. We take a taxi back to Claremont and walk into Café D'Capo on Main Road. They have this special there we can afford, and so we order two bottles of wine and polish them off over a large margherita.

Then we order another bottle.

During intervals, I look across the road to where I could buy airtime. Ruan says he knows a guy who lives in a flat in the same building as the café; that he can pat him down for a *bankie*, about three grams of cheese.

We take the lift up. The guy holding the *bankie*'s called Arnold. He comes out in silk boxers, with tousled hair, a boom of down-tempo beats pounding out of his living room. Ruan hands him three five-tigers for the weed, and calls him an overpriced but reliable asshole. They share a forced, stilted laugh, and then we take the lift back down.

We walk past Café D'Capo, waving guiltily at the waitress clearing our table. She looks twice our age, and has our soiled serviettes bunched in her hands. We cross the road and wait for a taxi at the corner of Cavendish Square, just across the road from the Nando's. I decide against walking into the mall for airtime. I can get it later, I decide, maybe further along the way.

What? Ruan says to us, after a while.

We've been staring at him since we bought the weed from Arnold.

Dude, I know him from a guy at work, he says.

We grin. Cissie and I don't say anything. We nod and look across the road.

Then Cissie says, what do you think of guys like that, anyway? He probably has parents who own half of Cape Town.

I shrug. Maybe I should send him my CV, I say.

Then our taxi arrives. The *gaartjie* leaps out, hefting stacks of coins in a canvas sack, a white Sanlam moneybag that's gone brown around the bottom stitching. He points us towards the taxi and we pile in before the door slides shut on its own.

Inside the Hi-Ace, I take Ruan's cellphone and SMS *Yes* in response to my uncle Vuyo's message. Then, to sign it, I write Lindanathi and attach my number for him to reply to. I resist an urge to turn my phone off. If this is what he wants, then this is what he wants, I decide. I hand the phone back to Ruan.

The three of us spend the next hour putting up posters along the main road, from Claremont to Salt River, all of them telling people how to buy my ARVs from me. Then we carry glue in Tupperware containers from Cissie's fridge, jump the Mowbray train to the city and take a bus out to the West Coast. I take a look at the time on my phone and it's only mid-afternoon. I guess this is what they mean when they call Cape Town the city of slumber. Time seems to speed up here, and then it stalls, and then it seems to speed up again before it stalls.

We pass Paarden Eiland just as the sun begins to burn itself through the clouds. It throws down a harsh beam that bisects the bus and Cissie taps my shoulder and says I should turn around. She tells me to look at how we're sitting on the right side of the light.

Then we pass Milnerton, the ocean sparkling and still, covered in white spots flecked across its vast surface. It looks as if all the salt has been sucked up to the lid of the Atlantic. After that Blouberg, the destination we've chosen for our excursion today, lists into our bus-driver's wind-screen.

I open the notebook program on my cellphone. I have orders for Ronny, Lenard and Leonardo. I've got one for Millicent. I write down Ta Lloyd and add a question mark after his name. Then, after a moment, I also add Nandipha, his wife. This makes up the list of reactives we could still sell our pills to at Wynberg. Two previous clients, Gerald and Melanie, haven't come to meetings for a year.

In Blouberg, we stalk into an internet café, this gamer-powered cavern complete with a coffee plunger and blue carpet tiles. The computers are sectioned into black cubicles with little hooks that hold up oversized headphones.

It's one of those LAN gamer killing pens, I say to Cissie. The first-person-shooter covens that seem to grow in popularity each year.

Cissie nods, somewhat slackened by the place's distractions. I fax my attendance slip to Sis' Thobeka at the front counter. There's a sign here that says they sell R29 airtime vouchers.

I catch Ruan looking around with this grim, beaten-up expression on his face.

He approaches the counter. I was such a frightened little shit when I was in high school, he says, shaking his head.

The voice he uses doesn't sound like him. It sounds as if it's only meant for his ears, not all six of ours, and when he's done, he looks up at us with a wan smile. Ruan doesn't like the year we've stepped into, and behind him Cissie takes note of this and raises her eyebrows. Not every story begs to be told, she seems to say.

I get the airtime and we walk out.

This is beach weather, almost, Cissie says, when we step outside. She stretches her arms out in front of her to feel the rays for evidence, but the solar system contradicts her. She drops her arms back down.

Well, half of almost, she says, correcting herself.

Ruan and I nod. It's a fitting description. Cissie has a way of sounding concise in the face of disapproval, and as if to defy the weather's indifference to her will, the three of us trudge into the Milky Lane up the road, next to the Total garage that ends the strip. We buy a vanilla milkshake and a pair of peanut-butter waffles and cross the road to Blouberg beach, stepping over the wooden railing and walking down a short pier to a grassy knot on the sand, not far from the polluted dunes. A large crane ship slowly drifts past the vista of Table Mountain, while above us, the sky clears up in a rounded blue column, spilling down enough light to make the ocean water blinding.

Ruan opens up our boxed packages. He uses a plastic knife to cut up the waffles while Cissie rolls a joint from the section Arnold sold us. She licks it from the tip to the gerrick and lights it with a copper Zippo from her shirt pocket. She holds in a drag, sipping the air in tiny increments, and then passes the joint on to me as she exhales.

Taking it from her, I lean back. The air feels cool but pleasant on my skin, and when I look out at the water, it seems to ripple in slow undulations, each one extending to the farthest reaches of the world.

I close my eyes and take a drag.

I try to savor the smoke's effect on my nervous system.

You know, Ruan says, his voice reaching me from behind my closed eyelids, Napoleon sent some of his troops to fight against a British fleet here. It happened in the nineteenth century, I think. More than five hundred people died.

I open my eyes. Ruan sits facing out to sea. He scratches his neck, takes a bite from his waffle, and leans back on his elbows. I pass him the joint.

Imagine, he says.

Imagine what?

Like, where we're sitting now could be the exact place some British or French assholes drove bayonets into each other. Isn't that weird?

I guess. That's probably this entire country, I say.

No, really, he says. Imagine. One guy could be standing with his boot on another's face, just over here, pushing the barrel of his musket down his throat and shouting, hey! We found the natives first! Then the other would be over there, going, *non! Niquer ta mère!*

Ruan does the accent well and Cissie and I laugh.

Hey, she says. I didn't know about that Blouberg and Napoleon thing. Do you think I could talk about it with the kids?

Sure, Ruan says. Make it a musket adventure.

He peels off a slice from the waffle and bites into it, sloppily. Then he grunts at us through the batter like a Disney pirate.

Cissie laughs.

Wait, she says. I didn't tell you guys about what happened to me last week, did I? Well, I made my kids draw me a picture of the Earth. Or I asked them to, anyway. Can you believe it? None of them knows what their planet looks like.

This isn't new. Cissie likes to think everyone has an opinion on outer space.

It doesn't take her long before she starts telling us about Cape Canaveral again.

If you know anything at all about Cecelia, then you'll know this isn't her first time on the subject. The three of us stretch out on the polluted sand, our fingers digging shallow troughs in Blouberg's white, heated dunes, and Cissie tells us about the headland on the Space Coast, the Cape in Florida, where the United States launches more than half of its space missions into orbit. Then she moves on to the Kennedy Space Center and tells us about the collective unconscious, the embedded memory all of us humans share with our planet. She tells us how she feels like she's been there at some point in her life, crossing an empty parking lot in Jetty Park, or lying under a clear sky and drinking a molten smoothie, or kicking around a bottle cap, or standing within touching distance of the station and staring out at the launch sites. The details don't matter, she says. The way Cissie thinks about her kinship with the headland, she tells us, isn't because she visited a family friend on the Florida coast when she was twelve, it's because everyone on our planet has a story to share about space. It's the only thing she's certain of, she says. That everyone has an idea about what the sky turns into at night.

Listening to her, I feel as I always do: uncertain. I have a feeling it might be true, but Ruan, on the other hand, is adamant he doesn't have a story about space.

I watch him pull on what's left of the roach and bury the ember in the sand. Cissie tears off a corner from a waffle and pushes it into her mouth, chewing on it for a long time before sucking the syrup off her fingers. We don't eat the banana slices. I watch them pile up in the red boxes for later.

I roll another joint. When I look up to lick it, a container ship makes its way into our view from the horizon. Then Cissie asks me to tell her a space story.

I don't have one, I say.

Unfazed, she leans over and hands me her lighter. Then she draws back and says, of course you do. Everyone does.

I look ahead. I can feel my elbows digging holes in the sand. I flip the copper lid of the lighter and torch the joint at its pointed end. It burns slowly and I take a long drag before I let the smoke out through my nostrils in thick white plumes.

I'll work on it, I say.

Then the three of us go quiet for a while.

The sand under my feet feels packed. Closer now, the container ship sounds its horn, its bilge cleaving the water like a scalpel through skin. I watch as a handful of ships melt into the horizon, each one swaying before tipping over the edge of the world.

It's better outside those killing pens, Ruan says after a while, and I remember how his face looked inside the internet café.

Cissie and I don't answer him.

I lie back and watch my blood turn orange behind my eyelids. The grass spikes me between my ears and my neck, and the heave of the ocean, when it reaches us, sounds like the breathing of an asthmatic animal. We remain quiet a while longer, and I suppose it's now, with the column of blue finally closing up above us, and the water losing its shimmer and ability to gouge, that my eyelids turn from orange to red and then to black again, and Bhut' Vuyo, my uncle from Du Noon, sends me another text message, and this time around, he tells me in clear terms to come home to them.

SECOND PART

WHEN I KILL THE FIRST KID ON THE RUGBY FIELD, the first thought that goes through my head, besides having to release the trigger, is that somehow this isn't so bad. I mean, it's awful how the bullet—we're using a clip of half-jacketed hollow points—shatters his skull just above the ear and he falls down, blood splashing and hair fluttering, and I think to myself, after all, Harriet Tubman is also dead. Then Ruan peers over my shoulder, looking down at the blood sinking into the ant-filled grass. Nice headshot, he says to me. Then Cissie takes the gun from my hands and carelessly shoots another kid in the throat. I guess this one would've been the lock in the team: that's how high he jumps. His throat explodes into winglets of flesh and all three of us have to shut our eyes against the blood. I step forward and say to my friends, I don't know. I say, do you think this will work? Cissie hands me the gun and takes her shoes off. When the green grass spikes between her toes, she smiles, and I guess this is what killing for the government is like. The gun is slicked all over with sweat, and every time I blink, I see the world through a prism of blood. Then another kid falls and Ruan bends over his bleeding head and asks, why us though? If they're so good at killing, he says, then why don't they do it themselves? I tell him this isn't so much killing as it is cleaning up a mess. These kids, all of them, they're already dead. Cissie says it's eerie and we both ask her, what is? She says, gunshots with no sirens. Then Ruan and I look up at her through the sound of the day's rising traffic. Cissie opens her mouth again, as if to say something further, but when her lips close in silence, I wake up in the bathroom at work.

My back cramps on the toilet seat. I lean over and try to stretch it. Then I take two more painkillers and look down at the space between my legs. In the dim light, my phone blinks blue before going off again. This indicates the arrival of a new message.

I hear my colleague Dean stumble into the next stall. His knees drop on the floor and he starts to heave, the room filling up with the smell of vomit. Without fail, Dean brings a hangover to work with him on Sunday shifts. Saturday nights, he plays drums for the house band at The Purple Turtle, a popular punk bar in the middle of Long Street. The owner, a Rastafarian named Levi, keeps half the earnings the bands bring in for him at the door. He compensates for this by keeping a bar tab open for the performers when they finish a set. I stand on the toilet seat and give Dean the rest of my painkillers. Then I sit back down and press a button to take my phone off standby.

Ruan maintains the email account we use for orders. The new message, cc'd to Cissie, is about a bulk order. I open it and read the MMS on the toilet seat.

It's one paragraph long, and it doesn't have a lot to describe. The client says he'll buy everything off us, paying us double for the order. He doesn't want any parcels or messengers, he specifies; we have to meet him in person or there's no deal. I read it twice and look at my phone for another moment. Then I flush the toilet and rinse my hands off at the sink.

On my way out, Dean looks up from his open stall and thanks me.

Dude, really, he says, and I nod.

His blond hair sticks to the sweat on his forehead, and he sits crumpled on the floor. He's wearing an old torn Pantera shirt. I reach for the handle and shut him in.

Then I walk back out to work.

I have this job I guess I should've mentioned. I work in Green Point, at a DVD rental store—the Movie Monocle—and I clock in every Sunday to Wednesday. The money from the orders Ruan, Cissie and I take in, as well as the allowance I receive as compensation for what happened to me all those years ago at Tech, is enough to keep me on my feet when my landlord calls me at the end of each month.

What they have me do here is stand behind a low vinyl counter—a hollowed-out semi-circle—where I become captain in my black shirt and orange cap, taking in rolled-up twenties and membership cards from the patrons of the Movie Monocle. This is where you'll find me. Whenever I look up from my hands, I can see movie posters lined up against the yellow walls, about three meters above the gray carpet tiles, each one touching the edges of the next. Directly in front of me, two ceiling fans whop the air, equidistant from my counter and the back wall.

I dry my hands on my jeans before I settle myself behind the counter. Then I take another look at Ruan's email. I press reply and ask Cissie and Ruan if this client isn't a cop.

They don't answer me for a while. Then Cissie sends back a reply: I hold reservations about thinking it's a cop thing...

I wait for her to finish.

She writes, I mean, guys, we shouldn't panic right away, should we? This could just be someone's idea of a bad joke, right?

I sigh.

On Sundays, Cissie takes a train out to visit her aunt in a nursing home in Muizenberg. She uses this time to ease herself into a gentle comedown. In order to organize her body's depletion of dopamine, and to quell her unease about mortality, Cissie surrounds herself with aging bodies.

In an octagonal courtyard, she and her aunt pick out grass

stalks which they knit into small bows and wreaths. This is where I imagine her now: lying on her back and typing with the sun in her face.

I decide to let it go. Then I get a message from Ruan.

I had the same thought about the police, he says.

This doesn't surprise me, either. Like me, Ruan rarely shares a moment of Cissie's tranquility. He gets comedowns no worse and no better than anyone else. Sundays for him just mean another computer in another room. He tells me he knows where I'm coming from.

I'm about to scroll down when I hear the storeroom door open. I slip my phone in my pocket and place my hands on the counter. I try to keep my back straight.

My manager appears from the door in the far wall, holding up a plastic clipboard.

That's it, keep smiling, he tells me.

I nod.

Until two months ago, Clifton was just another peon who worked the counter here at the Monocle. He got promoted after Red, our last manager, gave notice and moved to Knysna. Clifton's been giving us orders ever since. I wait for him to turn the other way before I pull out my phone.

Placing it on the counter, I read the rest of the message from Ruan.

This guy isn't a cop, he says, but he knows who we are.

He forwards Cissie and me a new mail. We each take a moment to read it. The message was delivered by the client at noon. It includes our names, where we live and where we work, and at the bottom it says, I am not the police. Then the client tells us he'll pay us first. We can decide what we want after that.

Meaning we can just take the money, am I right? Cissie says.

I'm about to answer her when I hear Clifton meandering into our store's Action section. He's run out of things to do again. He raises his clipboard and scratches the back of his neck, powdering his black collar with a mist of dandruff. I go back to my phone.

To Ruan and Cissie: okay, what's going on here?

Neither of them replies for close to a minute and I start to feel concerned. This returns me to Bhut' Vuyo, and on impulse I open my uncle's second message. I'm about to reply when Clifton raps his knuckles on the counter.

Hey, he says, there's no sleeping on the job.

I nod.

No chatting on the phone, either.

I close the text from my uncle and put the phone away.

Good, he says.

I watch Clifton turn his head towards the unit we've got mounted above the counter. Slowly, his face pinches inward.

Jesus, *okes*, he says. This is not on. This won't work at all.

I turn and look up at the unit. It's a black-and-white horror movie Dean's put on mute. Cornered by a hideous monster, a young woman backs up against a dungeon wall.

Clifton shakes his head. Guys, come on, he says. This isn't appropriate. You know what the rules are for the DVD.

I tell him it isn't my fault, everything was on when I came in.

Sure it was, he says.

The woman is now naked, lying in a puddle of black blood. Clifton walks around to my side of the counter, squeezes past me, and turns it off.

He sighs. Where's Dean?

He's in the bathroom, I say.

Great. You leave, and he enters. Do you plan it like this?

Maybe.

Clifton presses his clipboard against his chest, scowling like a sitcom villain. I watch him as he stomps off to hassle Dean in the lav. Then I look back down at my phone.

I've just received a notification SMS from the bank, Ruan says.

He tells us it's a deposit, and when he types out the amount, I stare at my phone for a while, making sure I'm parsing the figure right.

The client wants to meet up no later than today, Ruan says. He's scheduled the meeting at Champs, a pool bar next to the railway station in Mowbray.

I nod, but I have to scroll back up to the figure.

In the end, Cissie recovers from the shock before I do. She asks Ruan for a description of the client, a way to locate him inside the bar.

On his side, Ruan takes a moment to pass the question on and the three of us wait for the man to respond. Eventually, he types back to say we should look for the ugliest man in the bar. I wait for Ruan to explain, but he doesn't say anything further.

Then, all at once, I feel done at the Monocle. For the first time since I signed on with them, about a year ago now, I don't wait for my hours to arrive at their official cut-off point, or even for Clifton, my new ex-manager, to come back from scolding Dean inside the bathroom. I turn around and switch the DVD player back on. Then I drop my orange cap on the counter and walk out, making my way to the taxi rank on the station deck above Strand.

I cross over the short steel bridge and buy a packet of Niknaks. Then I walk to the bay marked for Claremont. Inside the taxi, I lean my head against the glass and watch as a pink band wraps itself around the sky over Cape Town—from Maitland to Athlone—and a haze of pollution simmers over the land beneath it. I can feel the cogs of the city's industries churning down to stillness, and smell the exhaust fumes from the taxis, as if each plume was mixing in with our exhaustion.

On the main road, I decide to put my uncle out of my mind. With the money to consider, this seems a reasonable measure to take. Existence goes on as we all navigate our need for currency.

Even Bhut' Vuyo would understand this. He needs money as much as anyone else. Or maybe, I think, he needs it more.

In Newlands, I find Ruan waiting by the gate, pushing up against the wire fence around Cissie's building. Cissie isn't back from her pilgrimage to Muizenberg yet, and by the way Ruan looks, I can't tell if he's high or coming down. I join him on the pavement.

Ruan, you have this face on I think you should see.

He shrugs. Is Cissie still in Muizenberg?

I nod.

I need to find an old person, Ruan says. He tries to laugh, bunching his shoulders together, but the feeling doesn't last. You don't always get to ward off exhaustion, huffing Industrial the way we do.

I lean my back into the fence.

Ruan pulls out a half-smoked cigarette from his pocket and lights it with a broken matchstick. Then he cups a hand over the flame and waves the match out before chucking it into the garden. I watch him sigh and drop his shoulders before taking a drag.

Man, he says, breathing out smoke. When I saw that money coming in, I just started shaking. I was at my place, right? And I had to stop typing for a while. I mean, Jesus, Nathi. He pauses and looks up the road. When's the new shipment coming in?

In a day or two, I say.

Ruan nods. Of course I told the client it was short notice, he says. The guy said it was fine, you know, that today was just a meeting between friends. Can you believe that? He called us friends.

Ruan's cheeks pull inward as he drags on his cigarette, his fingers pinching the sponge as thin as an envelope. I watch the carcinogens leaking out of his body.

I guess we've all tried to pack in the filters. We even came close last year, when we decided to quit nicotine and move out of the city entirely. Our plan was to relocate with our pill money to the Eastern Cape, where we'd harvest khat near the Kei River and hike the valley gorge that curves like a wide vein between Bolo and Cathcart. We didn't plan for long: before the end of the month, we heard reports of how a van, loaded with a boxful of stems, was stopped with bullets on its way to King William's Town. The urge died in us after that.

Ruan blows out another gray fog from his insides. He passes me the cigarette and I take a short pull, blowing smoke through my nose and through the fence.

The two of us stand in silence as the wind fusses the trees around West Ridge, its force snapping off the winter leaves and blanketing the curb in brown and orange patterns. We watch them scrub without noise against the rutted tar.

Then Ruan breaks through our silence.

This ugly description, he says.

I listen. I flick my cigarette on the tar and turn to face him.

Do you think it's code for something?

Maybe, I say. I don't know. It could be a word for dangerous.

Scars, Ruan says.

Then we fall into more silence.

I turn and hook my fingers on the mesh fence, hanging my weight on the sagging wire. I used to cross my eyes on fences like this when I was a child, a private trick that could make the holes in the squares leap out like holograms, but when I try it now, the optical illusion hurts my eyes. I uncross them and watch as the wind pushes against a green cardboard box, turning it over between the bins in the far corner of the parking lot. It knocks over a brown beer bottle, a quart balanced against the wall, and causes it to spew out frothy dregs, the foam washing across a fading parking line.

Cissie says all this silence in Newlands isn't a coincidence, that her whole neighborhood's haunted. The suburb's built on a grave site, she says, the plot of a man called Helperus Van Lier: an eighteenth-century evangelist who lived in the Dutch Cape Colony. Cissie says piety has the ability to flow inside tap water, and that even plant life isn't safe from Calvinist ghosts. This is the reason behind the stillness, she tells us, or at least why she owns a water filter.

There's something else I didn't show you, Ruan says.

I turn around.

I didn't tell you and Cissie this, but the client sent me copies of our ID's. He attached them in that email I sent you with our names and jobs on it, remember, but you know how Cissie's phone is. I had to take the jpegs off the MMS. Here, he says. Take a look at it.

I take his phone and start browsing through his images. It's true. We come up one after the other. The man did all three of our ID's in color.

Here's Ruan, here's Cecelia, and here I am.

Here's Russell, here's Evans, and here's Mda.

Ruan looks at me with his face pulled back in a wince, a form of apology. I look back down at the phone again.

Then up.

The thing is, he says.

I hand him his phone back. He slides it into his pocket.

The thing is, he says, it doesn't seem like we have much of a choice here. We have this guy's money, and we know that he's dangerous. He's not a cop, but he's got the reach of one. We know that he's free of the law, but we're not sure he's outside of it.

I nod. It isn't hard to see his point. By giving us his money, the client has us bound.

Of course, there can't be any police for us, either, Ruan says.

I nod again.

Look, Nathi, he says, I can't just walk into the bank and tell them to reverse the transaction, can I? I mean, we're lucky having that much money in the account hasn't raised any suspicion to begin with. Now what if I go in there and start tampering with it? Then what? That's a sure way of getting people to ask me things I have no answers for. The only option we have is to meet him.

He's right. I tell him I agree. Then I let another moment pass before I say I quit my job.

Ruan turns around. You quit?

I walked out before cashing up.

He takes a moment to look up the street. Maybe you'll find another one, he says.

I sigh. I guess he's trying to encourage me. Which is good. I could use more of that.

Jesus, Ruan says then. I did the same thing.

I turn to him, surprised. He falls back on the fence and knits his fingers together. Ruan stretches his arms out to crack the knuckles on each hand, and I notice an expression I've never seen on his face before. It reminds me of a game-show contestant I once saw as a child on a show called *Zama Zama*. The contestant, a man from the rural Eastern Cape, had directed a similar smile at the host, Nomsa Nene, at the crowd, and then finally at his family, after choosing the wrong key for the grand prize.

It was a shitty job, I say to him. When you told us about the money, I don't know. I just took my cap off and left. The strangest thing was that I hadn't even decided about accepting it. It just seemed like the right thing to do.

Ruan nods. I felt the same way about the firm, he says.

We go quiet over another cigarette. Ruan smokes it down to the filter and throws it away. Then he lights another one and I take it from him when he's done.

It's a favor, you know? To both myself and my uncle. He even spits, now, whenever he sees me in the office parking lot.

I nod. Ruan's told us this story before.

The company he works for lies in an old office park in Pinelands. Their building, one of fifty five-story units that face out to Ndabeni, an industrial suburb north of Maitland, came as a last resort to him. Early on, when Ruan started applying for posts as an assistant network administrator, he ruined his CV by losing three jobs in succession. The reason for dismissal was a slew of unforeseen panic attacks: from the copy machine to the kitchen area, he could be found curled up, or fainting on carpet tiles or buffed lino. Even though he always went back to work a week later with an apology, and sometimes a note from a doctor he'd paid to say it was epilepsy, he was always fired. Over the phone, even as his former employers expressed their sympathy and good wishes, they described him as too great a liability to keep on a payroll, and suggested he seek out a program for special care.

For a while, it felt as if there had been no options left open to him, and then—after a series of emails, all dispatched with great reluctance, but pushed by the pressure of an increasing interest rate—his uncle relented and put him on a conditional intern's contract. His uncle's oldest son had recently relocated to the UK, and this freed up the flat in Sea Point, where Ruan was to stay, paying rent into his uncle's account. This is what led to his present situation. Ruan's probation period extended itself to more than four years, and even though he renews his contract every twelve months, there's never any mention of a pay increase. This is how he still gives a lot of what he earns to his uncle and the bank.

I squash the cigarette ember with my toe and kick it towards the gutter. It rolls in a light breeze, stopping just shy of the pavement's lip.

I don't know if I thought of myself as having already taken the money, Ruan says. I just saw it there, when that SMS came, and I thought other things could happen.

I move away from the fence and settle myself on the edge of

the pavement. Ruan doesn't follow, and for a while the two of us speak without facing each other. Two cars drive past us and after they've gone, I notice a figure standing in the house opposite. I can't tell whether it's a man or a woman, but I can see them looking out at us through a veil of curtain lace. Eventually, when it seems like our eyes have met and locked for a long time, the figure takes a step back and draws the curtain closed between us. I lean back and feel the tar and pebbles digging into my palms.

Then I take a breath and decide to tell Ruan what I'm thinking.

The two of us, I say, we've already accepted the money from the client.

Ruan tells me that he knows we have. He sits down on the pavement next to me and kicks a pebble into the road. He says he hopes Cissie has, too.

It takes Cecelia another half an hour to return. The three of us take the lift to her flat, and as we do, she doesn't speak to me or Ruan.

Cissie walks into her kitchen and starts rifling through the cabinets. Then she crouches and opens the drawers beside the stove.

I'm looking for the Industrial, she says. In case anyone's interested.

Ruan and I take our seats on the living-room floor in silence, facing each other from the opposite ends of her coffee table.

My aunt died today, Cissie says. It happened just over an hour ago.

She dips her head back behind the counter, rifling through more cabinets. Then she opens a coffee tin and, finding it empty, lets it roll out of the kitchen.

It's weird, she says. First, we're picking twigs. Then I take the train and she's dead.

Cissie turns to the basin, plugs in a drain stopper and starts running the hot water. She removes a heap of cups and plates from the sink and stacks them on the dish rack. Then she draws back the short floral curtains and pushes the windows open to let in a gust of air. The water slams hard against the sink. She squeezes soap against the steam.

On the other side of the counter, Ruan and I watch.

Cissie whisks the soap to a lather with her hand. Then she closes the tap and flicks the foam off her fingers. The crazy thing is, she says, I almost didn't bother going today.

I return my eyes to my knees and notice a plastic bottle lying on its side under her table. I reach for it and find it still closed. Then I get up and hand it to her.

Cissie receives it with a nod, unscrews the lid and sniffs the top. She starts to huff and the bottle crinkles inward. Done, she leaves it to drop in the sink. She brushes both hands over her face. Then she arranges the plates on the dish rack.

The client, she says. When does he want to meet?

I look at Ruan. He keeps his eyes on his phone.

Tonight, he says.

Cissie nods. I want the money, she tells us.

Then she reaches for a dishcloth and dries her hands and elbows. She turns around.

Do you?

This is what she asks us.

Ruan and I fall silent for a moment. Then we answer her at the same time. We tell her that we do.

Cissie finds half a pack of Tramadol on her top shelf. She's kept it in an old Horlicks tin above the kitchen counter, saving it for a day like today. We split the pills over her glass coffee table. Then, while passing around a glass of water, Cissie gets a text message from Julian. It's about a Protest Party at his flat off Long Street. We take what's left of the pills.

Outside, the sky's grown dark again, thick and almost leaden in texture. To the north, columns of rain emerge from the hills that once came together, more than a million years ago, to create the crest and saddle of Devil's Peak. We smoke another cigarette with the painkillers. Then we wait for a taxi out on the main road. I get the feeling, as we do, that the sky could drop down on us at any moment.

Thankfully, the trip doesn't take long. The sky shows no interest in us, and we arrive at Julian's an hour later. Standing across the road from his place, I realize that my hours have become something foreign to me, that they've taken on a pattern I can no longer predict.

Looking out over the cobblestones on Greenmarket Square—each orb cut from a slab of industrial granite, connecting the cafés on the right with the Methodist Mission on Longmarket, where hawkers and traders from different sectors of the continent erect stalls and barter their impressions of Africa—I feel my thoughts branch out and scatter, grow as uncountable as the cobblestones beneath us, as if each thought were tied to every molecule that comprises me, each atom as it moves along its random course.

Ruan waves to the security guard. I ring Julian's intercom and we get buzzed to the eleventh floor. On our way up, we stand apart, the mirrors in the lift reflecting the fluorescent lights. We remain quiet, facing ourselves as our bodies get hauled through thick layers of concrete. I lean against the lift wall and think of Greenmarket Square again, and how, not too far from here, and less than two hundred years ago, beneath the wide shadow of the muted Groote Kerk, slaves were bought and sold on what became a wide slab of asphalt, a strip divided by red-brick islands and flanked by parking bays where drivers are charged by the hour; behind them, yesteryear's slave cells, which are now Art Deco hotels and fast-food outlets. I think of how, despite all this, on an architect's blueprints, the three of us would appear only as tiny icons inside the square of the lift shaft, each suspended in an expanse of concrete.

Then the lift doors slide open.

Cissie walks out of the lift and Ruan and I follow a step behind, trailing her down a long open walkway. We don't say anything else about her aunt. The three of us don't mention our meeting with the client, either. Instead, we reach Julian's flat in silence, propping ourselves up in front of his white door.

Cissie knocks.

Julian's door has a silver number: an eleven hundred with two missing zeroes. In the corridor, voices mill together in a growing murmur over the music, while shadows dance behind the dimpled window. Outside, a couple sits on the fire escape behind us, a few steps below the landing, holding bottles of Heineken and sharing a cigarette. Cissie and Ruan face straight ahead, focused on getting themselves inside the party. The music seems to get louder, too, and the weather grows colder, but that doesn't seem to bother us.

Loud footsteps approach on the other side of the door, and before long we hear someone struggling with the lock.

Looking back down, I notice that the couple, both in black winter jackets and thick woolen beanies, have a large cardboard cut-out leaning over the steel steps behind them. The placard bears a detailed illustration of the female anatomy.

Eventually, Julian manages to get his door open. He greets us from the threshold, his face painted bright silver. He's both tall and peppy tonight, so tall, in fact, that we have to look up to see his face. Smiling, he uses his long arms to wave us in.

Please, guys, he says, come inside.

Ruan, Cissie, and I file into the hallway and then into the kitchen. It's a small space, with brandy boxes lying flattened across the tiles. The three of us try to walk around them as Julian follows behind.

We went to a farm earlier, he says, waving his hand across

the kitchen counter. From one end to the other, the surface is packed with raw vegetables. Liquor bottles emerge intermittently from the grove.

Help yourselves, Julian says, and we do.

Cissie takes our quarts from me. We bought them with a bottle of wine at the Tops near Gardens. I keep the Merlot and rinse out three coffee mugs in the sink. The brown water inside the basin looks a day old, so I yank the plug-chain. Then I stand there for a moment, watching as the fluid swirls out.

I'm not surprised to find the drain half-clogged. I've been in and out of places like Julian's for most of my adult life. One year, Cissie brought a colleague over and we played Truth or Dare at West Ridge. On a Truth, I'd tried but failed to piece together how many times I'd woken up shoeless on someone's lidless toilet. Nicole, the colleague, had meant the question in good humor, but even as we all laughed, I remembered how most times, my eyes would be half-focused, the door swaying as my pants rode off my ankles.

Well, do you like it?

Julian breaks out in a laugh behind me. He points a finger at his chin and wipes a thumb across his forehead. The contrast between his face and his mascara makes his eyes appear pressed out, or even feral. Each orb bulges out in shock, as if from proptosis, a sign of an overactive thyroid, and a sometime symptom of the virus I have inside me. Standing in place, and swaying on his feet, Julian achieves an eerie trembling, as if he were a supporting character excerpted from a malfunctioning video game, now stranded in a different reality, awaiting instruction in our less tractable environment.

I don't know, Cissie says. She leans back against the counter.

On her right, Ruan pulls out a carrot and inspects it. He breaks off the stem and starts chewing. I open the bottle of wine and pour us each a coffee mug of Merlot. Then Julian starts laughing again. I look up and find him still swaying.

Think about this, he says. Under the kitchen light, his teeth shimmer like dentures. He waves his hands and tells us to listen.

We prepare to. I hand Ruan and Cissie their mugs and, taking a sip from my own, lean back and wait for him to start.

I'm doing something bigger than all my previous marches, Julian says.

I nod, sipping the Merlot. Ruan pulls out another carrot from the grove.

Cissie and I watch him as he yawns into his sleeve.

I suppose none of this is new to us. Julian hosts a party like this every second month now. He ends each of them the same way, too, by locking everyone inside his flat before morning. The reason he calls them protests is because the following day, he organizes his guests, a half-stoned mass, into a march outside the parliament gates. There, Julian takes pictures of them, which he then sells at a gallery in Woodstock.

Cissie used to be classmates with him. They attended the University of Cape Town together, both receiving MFA's from Michaelis, before Cissie became a teacher. I once read an interview Julian had given to the arts section of a local weekly. Towards the end, when the interviewer had asked him if his marches were protests in earnest or just performance art, he'd chosen to skip the question. Later, when I googled him, I found a one-minute clip of Julian playing a prank on his agent: he arrived at his exhibition disguised as one of the parking attendants working on Sir Lowry Road, in a green luminous vest and a cap slung low over his forehead. The gallery walls held large framed photographs of his marches, and the video ended with Julian wearing a wine-stained paper cup on his head.

I'll tell you all about it later, he says. You'll be around, right?

We might be, Cissie says.

Sure, he tells her. We'll talk then.

I pour out more wine for us, and find a shelf for our beer

inside the fridge. Holding our coffee mugs, the three of us walk out into the living room.

In the lounge, Ruan, Cissie, and I join an audience for Julian's latest performance. Everyone else draws closer to watch, and Julian presents himself as our party host, kneeling down in front of us. Smiling from the head of the coffee table, his metal face gleams while a string of sweat drips down the bridge of his nose. He removes a button pin from his blazer and turns it over to take out the fifteen tabs of LSD he's concealed in the back. Then he returns his hands to his pockets and tells everyone they should know what to do by now.

They nod.

Ruan, Cissie, and I keep still. We watch as Julian's followers gather around the coffee table, each of them with their head bowed. In order, they raise their left hands and Julian nods as he passes them the acid.

Cissie pulls on my sleeve. Let's go, she says.

I nod.

Ruan pulls on the sliding door at the end of the living room. Then the three of us walk out onto the balcony.

I have very little regard for Nietzsche's detractors.

This comes from a guy sitting on the floor. He has his legs spread out in a narrow V over Julian's tiles. He introduces him-self as an ecology student. He's wearing a fitted leather jacket under a black balaclava that covers his face, and he's speaking to a girl leaning against the balcony wall. The girl laughs at his quip. I'm doing my third year in linguistics, she says.

We share a marijuana cigarette with them. Then it's followed by a leaking pipe we take a pass on. On the balcony, the breeze feels tactile around our fingertips. We take hits from the weed and sip on our wine. From where we're standing, our view of Cape Town is a maze of brick walls; a checkerboard of aban-doned office lights. Exhaust fumes waft up from the streets below, mixing with the smell of rubber baked during the day, a combination that reminds me of Ruan's summation of our planet's atmosphere: that the ozone layer is Earth's giant garbage lid.

Julian looks like a deep-water mutant, Ruan says.

Cissie and I laugh. I inhale and blow out smoke.

To defend herself against the cold, Cissie's wearing a green hoodie. The strings on the sides are pulled and knotted under her chin. She leans out over the balcony.

You know, Julian asked about my documentary, she says.

Cissie has an audio documentary she edits for two hours each month. The subject is a twenty-eight-year-old from Langa called Thobile. Last year, Thobile quit his job to live on eight rand a day. It was in solidarity with his community, he said, and in the clips Cissie played back for us at West Ridge, we could hear the difference in his tone at the beginning of the experiment, and then a month later. Cissie, who planned to paint a portrait of him—using only her memory and her recording as a guide—said he lost eight kilograms in three weeks.

Leaning on the railing, I turn to face her. How's it going? I say.

Cissie shrugs. I don't know. They all started getting sick.

I remember listening to Thobile in the clips Cissie played for us. He described how he hadn't robbed anyone, yet.

He has this little brother, you know. In June, Vuyisa contracted bronchitis. That's why Thobile had to go back to work.

I nod.

Cissie digs in her pocket and retrieves a soft pack of filters. The two of us watch as a car speeds down the narrow lane below. Its headlights illuminate a piece of graffiti on the opposite wall: PLEASE DON'T FEED THE ANIMALS.

You know, Cissie says, I don't mind my job.

Since our wine is almost finished, we drink what's left of it in shallow sips.

No, really, she says, but there's all this shit in between. I mean, what are we even doing here? My aunt died today, Cissie says, and here I am, standing on a balcony, listening to people talk shit about Nietzsche.

Ruan looks over her shoulder. Loud enough for the ecology student to hear, he says, Nietzsche's the Nazi one, isn't he?

On the floor, the student shrugs under his balaclava. The leaking pipe is laced with methamphetamine. I start to feel awake when I try a hit. My pulse begins to pick up and I turn to Ruan. Then I decide to tell Cissie about my job.

When I'm done, Cissie releases the rail and takes a long drag from her cigarette.

Then she tells me that's good. She says to me, now we have to go to Mowbray.

Julian spots us making our way down the wood-paneled hallway. Maybe it's his new eyes. He follows after Ruan and raises his arms.

You can't be leaving, he says.

We are, Cissie tells him.

I haven't even thought of doing the lock-up yet.

Well, something came up, she says.

Julian shakes his head. He walks past us and starts working the latch.

I get it, he says, you're a team. I like that.

We watch him struggle over the lock for a while.

I get the feeling that I don't mind waiting here. I can still hear the laughter coming in from Julian's balcony. It rings over the music. When I look over Ruan's shoulder, I notice the ecologist and linguist walking back inside, hand in hand, both of them giggling and shaky on their feet. The ecologist moves in towards her and they kiss. The two of them stand like that for a while, wobbling, kissing and keeping each other in balance. Then Julian gets the door to unlock and holds it open for us.

We file out onto the walkway.

The other couple comes running up from the fire escape.

The girl carries their placard like a crucifix. Dude, she laughs, you almost locked us out.

She pushes past Julian and the guy from the landing trails behind her.

I turn around and jog towards Cissie and Ruan. They've walked ahead to the lift, where they're holding it open and waiting.

Inside, when the doors draw shut, the laughter from the flat fades again, and the three of us watch ourselves in the mirrors once more. Cissie inches towards me, and without speaking, she places her head flat against my shoulder. Then the lift grumbles, and a few floors down, she says, there's nothing to envy about this place or the people inside it.

I nod. Then I look up at the silver ceiling and watch as the fluorescent light falls on her hair. Cissie's hand clutches my shoulder as we reach the ground floor.

The three of us sit side by side inside a taxi headed out to Mowbray. Up front, behind a cracked windscreen and a GET RICH OR DIE TRYING sticker, our driver shifts his stick up another gear and we hurtle through Woodstock with rising speed, the Hi-Ace gliding past a U-Save store, a hair salon and an internet café that pawns second-hand jewelry.

I can't control my thinking, again, Cissie says.

From our seats, Ruan and I watch her scratch the bridge of her nose. Then Cissie takes off her green hoodie and says, my head's doing this thing where my aunt isn't dead yet.

I don't think I want it to be doing that, she says.

We drive past another U-Save store. Then Cissie tells us this is how her thinking turned when her mother died of stomach cancer when she was twelve.

This isn't about either one of them, though, she adds.

I nod at her. Then I turn to look out at the road.

Through my window, the sky looks dull and impenetrable, like the screen of a malfunctioning cellphone. I imagine it made of plastic, each corner suppressing the passage of vital information. Perhaps we've all come to malfunction this way. Perhaps language, having once begun as a system of indistinct symbols, would never develop beyond what we knew, but instead, would continue to function as a barrier between ourselves and others.

I'm not sure what to tell her.

I circle my hand around the fingers she's left on my thigh.

Then our driver stops just before we list into Obs, dropping off an elderly couple who only paid enough to get as far as Salt River. The door slides shut and we move down the main road again.

On my right, Cissie says, we need to make a plan. She widens her eyes and says we need a strategy on how we're ending our lives, tonight.

Ruan and I laugh.

Or at least we try to.

I thought I could go in first, I say. You guys could wait for me outside the bar. I remind them that after all, I'm the one who's halfway dead.

They nod, but neither one of them laughs.

I tell them I think we need a strategy for how we talk to him. We should give out as little information as we can, I say.

Ruan and Cissie nod.

Then our taxi pulls over at the McDonald's in Obs. A few people get off, and the *gaartjie* leaps out and calls for more passengers. He shouts out Claremont, Wynberg, and then repeats it. I watch him cross over the main road, searching for passengers leaving St Peter's Square. The sky seems to darken as the minutes pass, and, turning back, I tell my friends I can't think of anything else.

Dude, I'm sold, Ruan says.

He seems nervous. This is how Ruan talks when he's nervous. I watch him pound a fist into his palm.

Then Cissie nods. I mean, what else is there to do?

She's right. There's nothing else we can do, I say.

The worst thing that can happen in this story, Cissie says, is that someone dies, and that's already kind of happened, hasn't it?

From across the road, the *gaartjie* calls for Claremont.

He doesn't look much older than us. He's wearing blue over-all pants and a black woolen beanie. I watch him skip between shoppers. He offers to help carry their packages.

On Station Road, we get off and walk past three lit-up hair salons on the main road. Most of the salons are still open in this area, even this late in the evening. Their windows throw yellow puddles of light onto the curb, drawing us a path to the four-way stop at Shoprite: a blurry line that changes this part of town into another suburb, before Rosebank becomes Rondebosch. We head east just before the police station, down St Peter's Road. We find Champs on the right, close to the bend. It has wide window panes with white vinyl letters on the glass. There's an eight-ball pattern on each side of the door.

We start off at the bar. Ruan and Cissie take seats on the high stools near the entrance; I step out to buy a filter from a vendor outside.

Somalia, he tells me, when I ask him where he's from.

The sound of the traffic mixes with the conversation of the pedestrians behind us, and we face each other across the scarred surface of his wooden cart. He's a thin man, wearing a kufi cap. I haggle him down to one rand fifty, but he has no change, he tells me, so I let him keep the two rand. Under the streetlight, I feel my buzz begin to fade, but when I ask him for khat, he shrugs and shakes his head. Then he starts to pack his wares, and as I watch him push his cart up the main road, I begin to suspect that being here might be a trap. Maybe Bhut' Vuyo knows I can be lured with money. That I have a price and I'm easy to find. I walk inside the bar. The smell of stale smoke clutches me like a glove.

We sit facing the packed beer fridges. The vodka and brandy bottles reflect the dim light, and my eyes feel dry as they glide over the whiskey and sherry. Green swathes fall across the counter in a soft pattern, the result of a soccer match playing on the sets.

I use my sleeve to wipe the sweat off my temples. I can hear my heart tapping inside my chest. I recall what I know about the pharmacology of *tik*: in one of Olive's stories, a baby was born with its intestines unspooled outside its body.

Maybe we should get a drink, Cissie says.

I lean forward and raise my hand for help. The woman tending the bar smiles under a helmet of bleached hair. We watch her standing at the other end of the counter, her back turned to us. From our place at the bar, we can see her texting on her phone. Now and then, she raises her head to laugh with a man in a cowboy hat. The man looks around fifty. He's wearing a white shirt under a brown suede blazer. On close inspection, his features are unremarkable, and I discount him as a candidate for our client. The match blares on a set above him: a game between Sundowns and Chiefs.

Our throats dry, the three of us fall silent. We spend the next minute leaning over the counter. I remind myself to take in normal breaths, which reminds me of Olive: the damage that makes her throat whistle.

What would you drink on your last day on Earth?

This comes from Cecelia, and it's timely as always.

She says, what if Last Life was moved up to now?

Ruan and I take a while to answer. Cissie plays with the strings under her chin.

I don't know, Ruan says eventually.

I don't either, I tell her. Maybe it is now.

The bartender works the other end of the bar. She's wearing a blue halter top over a pair of stonewashed jeans, and her short legs drag her feet across the floor. She serves the man in the hat another brandy and he beams at her.

I don't think I have any more money on me, I say.

Me neither, Cissie says.

Ruan pats his pockets. I might, he says.

Eventually, the bartender sees him waving. She approaches us, using one hand to wipe down the counter while the other holds up her phone. When she comes to a stop in front of him, Ruan takes out his money and places it on the rubber spill mat. It's enough for three quarts of beer.

We take small sips from the tall brown bottles. I swivel on my chair to catalog the patrons present at Champs. I try to convince myself that our client isn't here: that he would've approached us by now. Or we would've noticed him. Then I take another sip.

The bartender returns with Ruan's change, a combination of green notes and bronze coins. Placing the money on the counter, she pauses and looks up from her phone.

He's upstairs, she says.

The three of us look up and the bartender sighs.

The man, she says, turning to me, the strange one, the handicap. He told me to tell you he's waiting for you upstairs. He has the floor blocked off, but you can tell Vincent at the door and he'll let you in. Tell him you're the three guests. He'll see your friends, anyway, she says, pointing at Cissie and Ruan. Then she shrugs, done with her message.

I thank her as she sends another text from her phone. She doesn't respond, and I watch her walk back to the man in the cowboy hat, who orders another brandy.

Jesus, Ruan says, this guy booked the whole floor.

The whole floor, Cissie echoes.

My brain gives me nothing to add to this, so I ask them if we should finish our beer or take it up with us.

We need to revise our strategy, Ruan says.

Yes, we need to do that, Cissie says. Let's decide on a plan.

I tell them again that we shouldn't volunteer any information.

Ruan asks if we should mention seeing the money.

Not until he mentions it first, I say.

Then Cissie takes a long sip from her beer and we do the same. Fuck it, she says. What can he do to us here? She pushes back from the counter. This is a public place, isn't it?

It is. We've really done all we can to prepare, I say.

Ruan agrees, and in my head, I think: if he's Bhut' Vuyo then he's Bhut' Vuyo.

We just have to keep a cool head with him, I say.

Right, Ruan says. He gets up and stretches his arms. I need to take a leak. Don't sneak off without me.

Like you'd mind that, Cissie says.

Then Ruan takes a gulp from his quart, and, wiping the foam off his lips, stalks off to the bathroom. Left behind, Cissie and I slouch on our seats.

During a free kick, she turns to me and says, be honest, Nathi, are you afraid?

I tell her honestly, I don't know.

Me neither, she says. I have no idea what to think any more.

I got stabbed once, I tell her.

Really? Where?

I was in Obs.

The ghouls gathered around the plasma screen roar at another missed goal. For a while, Cissie and I drink in silence. Then Ruan comes back and leans on the counter.

He sighs.

I'm ready, he says, clasping his hands together.

He takes another sip from his beer, and when he's done, I say we should go up and see what happens to us. Ruan and Cissie try to laugh, but it doesn't last long. I can tell it's only to humor me.

We leave the counter just as the game hits half-time. The

soccer louts rush back to the bar, each of them griping and cheering over their glasses of brandy. I guess it gets hard to pick them apart, sometimes, the winners and the losers, but in any case, the three of us don't stick around to find out who's who.

We take our beers and walk up the staircase next to the men's room, where we find Vincent, the resident bouncer, arranging his face into a scowl. To get a clear image of Vincent, you'd have to imagine five slabs of braaied beef, all arranged in a pile and wrapped up in a beanie and a black dress shirt. Then you'd have to think of a pair of black jeans and black desert boots. None of them new, but pressed and buffed to look it.

I slow my friends down. Keeping myself at a distance, I tell the bouncer that it's us and that we're here for a meeting.

Vincent looks dubious.

He faces down and creases his brow. Naturally, he asks me who we are.

We're here to see the guy, I say, and point at the door.

He eyeballs us. Prove it, he says. Vincent centers himself in front of the door. I guess it's a bouncer maneuver or something.

I look at him and all I can think of is, whatever, I concede.

I tell Vincent we're here for hospital work; that we're working in the field as volunteers. The three of us, I say, we've all got jobs in a ward at Groote Schuur. That's what we have to talk about with the man inside. We're consulting.

He clicks his tongue. Consulting, he says. Still staring at us, Vincent raises a beefy paw to his face and draws a slow, tight circle in front of his forehead.

Was his face eaten by pigs? he asks.

I don't know what to tell him. To my right, Ruan says we can't disclose that.

Then Vincent nods. He sizes up Ruan before his eyes glide down to the quarts in our hands. Tell me, he says, what kind of hospital meeting is it where you have three children holding bottles of beer?

I sigh. I can't think of anything else.

Then the door cracks open and a woman approaches Vincent from behind. She lays a thin hand on his shoulder, and her voice flows out of her like a whisper.

Vincent, the man says to let them in, she says. You can collect your tip at the bottom till. Her hand drops and she disappears back into the room.

Vincent considers us a moment longer. Then, slowly, he starts to nod.

Okay, he says. You've convinced me. Feigning reluctance, but clearly pleased by his tip, he opens the door to the upstairs bar and waves us in like a butler.

Ruan, Cissie and I step over the threshold one after the other. Then we stand there holding our quarts, our eyes adjusting to the dimness.

I realize I've stopped breathing. That's when I hear his voice.

Please lock the door after you, he says. You'll soon learn how much I'm devoted to my people, but I'm afraid I'm not very fond of their intrusions.

It's strange, but when I hear him, I feel I have no choice but to do as he says. There's a strange, but commanding quality to the man's voice, and not only in volume, but also in texture. It has a metallic ring around its loudness, like a recording pushed through a speaker.

I take a shallow, faltering breath. Then I lock the door and trace his voice to a corner in the far left, where there's a silhouette of a man leaning back on one of the leather couches, one leg bent at the knee and crossed over the other. Above him, ribbons of smoke curl against the ceiling light, forming a mist in front of the windows overlooking St Peter's Road.

I'm over here, he says, waving his hand.

My head clears and my nausea thins out. I look through the room and locate his head, a long narrow face in silhouette against the large road-lit panes.

Please take a seat with me, he says.

Ruan, Cissie and I move towards him.

The woman behind the bar stares at us with a blank expression. She's also pressing the buttons on a cellphone. I watch its blue glow playing up her neck, a light that reveals a sharp jaw moving around a wad of gum. The three of us move past her.

You can't possibly still imagine I'm the law, the man laughs.

This is how he talks. He booms in a register that's picked out from two centuries ago. His tone sounds tired and tickled at the same time.

Ruan, Cissie and I find our seats opposite him at the low table.

Here we are, I guess.

Here's the ugly man. Here's our client.

He has his head down, his face covered in shadows. You get the feeling his features are nondescript, even in sunlight, and that his skull, closely shaven and dimly reflecting the street glow, looks like the skull of any other man. It's almost as if, in calling himself ugly, he's erased his features, drawing attention to something that isn't there. There's no way to describe him above the V of his white shirt. I lean back, confused.

Please allow me a moment, he says.

We do. We watch his fingers prod, fussing over a black PDA device on the coffee table. It's thick, about the size of my hand, and he's set it flat on its back. It's probably what he used to send us the emails, and the scanned IDs he intimidated us with. It has a dim screen light that illuminates only his wrists and cufflinks. More than once, he cracks the knuckles of his right hand as if in frustration at its speed or, I think to myself, as if to ground a stray current. Either way, I wouldn't be surprised.

The man clears his throat. He doesn't look up at us, but we watch him as he bunches his fingers around a stylus pen. He swipes a gray icon across the small screen.

I should tell you I'm rather pleased you were able to find your way to me, he says. I was beginning to wonder if I might've been the cause of too much trouble. I understand I called for us to meet at short notice and for that I should extend an apology, and believe me when I say I do. However, as you'll soon learn for yourselves, the matters which bring us together bear their own sensitivities regarding the dictates of time, and for that reason alone, I'm confident that our arrangement, as hasty or as modest as it might seem, is perhaps the one that could serve our purposes best.

Done, he pushes his PDA aside. Clicking open his gold cigarette case, he pauses for a moment. Then he weaves his head and trains his eyes through the dimness, raising his right hand to signal to the bartender.

My dear, he says, might we have the lights back on?

I hear the bartender closing her till. Her silhouette saunters around the counter and approaches the entrance. It turns a knob and a mist of yellow light settles over us.

Finally, here he is, I think to myself. He's wearing a three-piece suit, a deep red that matches the hat on the table. The hat is a long-brimmed fedora. It has a feather tucked inside the band.

This is when I realize what's unsettling me about his face. He's wearing a mask.

The man clears his throat and starts talking again.

You'd be shocked, he says, sounding both surprised and amused, how little science has accomplished for the facial prosthetic. The field's first and, by my humble estimate, truest visionary was a man born in the year of 1510. He was a Frenchman by the name of Ambroise Paré, who used to shear the hair off kings to earn his keep in the royal courts. He had as his regular clients Henry II, Charles IX and Henry III. Francis II is also said to have sat under his blade during his short kingship. In his work as a surgeon, however, he was a man at home on the battlefield. He made limbs for soldiers maimed during the wars, you see.

Here he pauses. He taps his cigarette filter on the gleaming case, his long fingers pushing the air out of the stick and compacting the tobacco leaves.

I see you've already helped yourselves to something to drink, he says. It's no bother, but should you want more, I beg you only to mention it. I should say, also, that Nolwazi here holds my vote as the best bar maiden this side of the mountain. He turns his head towards her, then back to us.

Now, he says, where was I? Oh, yes, we were discussing Ambroise Paré, weren't we?

He goes on like this. It turns out it's from the First World War, this mask he has on. That's what he tells us, anyway. He says nothing about his voice, but I can detect a hum whenever he takes a moment to breathe. I keep my eyes settled on his mask.

Well, he says, the technique itself is from the Great War. I'm afraid this hunk of tin isn't quite as old as that. You'll have to forgive me my indulgence. I tend to have a desire to get the face and mask out of the way as soon as I can. It's the only way I can guarantee myself anyone's attention. My face is somewhat of an attraction, you see. I myself am no stranger to its oddities. However, I invited you here for matters unrelated to my appearance. Now, friends, if you don't mind, may I?

He raises his hands to the sides of his face and holds them up against his ears. Ruan, Cissie and I sit with our hands by our sides, staring at him in silence.

The man's mask is painted the sandy color of his hands and his neck, with two round holes for eyes and two piercings at nose level for breathing holes. Just above the chin, it's carved into three narrow slits for him to speak through.

Cissie says, so there's a reason you didn't get plastic surgery?

This doesn't surprise us, me and Ruan, that Cissie would be the first to break through our silence.

I reach down for my beer again. The sip I take from the bottle tastes warm, and it causes my mouth to fill up with saliva. The bitterness clings to the sides of my tongue, trickling down my throat and knotting my stomach. I put the bottle back between my knees.

The man, as if noticing my discomfort, drops his hands.

He shakes his head and says, Monsieur Paré. The first men he patched up from the wars broke his big foolish heart. He gave them back their arms and legs and they took their own lives. They didn't favor their looks, you see. I've never understood those men. If you ask me, a man is given his scars as a consequence of his spirit, his battles out in the world.

He shakes his head, his answer to plastic surgery.

Then, following a brief pause, he says, now, I do trust I have your permission?

The man's hands pull at the sides of his mask and he lifts the tin off his face. Leaning back on the couch, with his arms set apart and his one leg over the other, his hands find the arm rests and his face reveals itself. If he's smiling, then none of us can tell.

Half his face appears burnt, the skinless meat gleaming in full view.

He's still facing us when the bartender walks over with a brandy snifter on a cloth-covered tray. The man nods at her and she disappears without a sound to sit behind the bar. He smokes his cigarette through a long white tube fitted into his throat, and half of the right side of his face is missing. The skin on the bottom half of his neck seems to lighten on its way down to his chest. It's a pattern that gives definition to how his larynx varies in relief. Tracing it down from his chin, it continues to rise as it descends, until it pushes itself taut against his skin, outlining the contour of a perfect cylinder.

The man watches me as I stare at him. Then he raises a hand to his neck.

Of course, I've had to adopt a more recent approach with my

voice. I find it rather important that one does what one can in order to be heard, don't you?

The flesh around his larynx vibrates when he speaks, and this is when I realize he has a machine humming against the walls of his throat. I look up.

You paid us a lot of money, I say. What for?

The man breathes out smoke through his nostrils. I'm under the impression my intention was clear, he says. I want to make a purchase.

We don't have any pills on us, I say.

He considers this and nods. I watch the smoke holding still around his face, like a meadow fog.

I figured as much, he says, unfazed. It was, after all, very short notice, as I've said. He inhales again and lets the smoke seep out.

I ask him, why did you bring us here?

Why, he says, you provide a social service, do you not?

It's a scam, I say.

The man laughs. He does that for a while.

Now, now, he says, we both know that isn't true.

He lifts one leg off the other and straightens himself up on the couch. Then he slips his cigarette case inside his jacket and reaches for his feathered hat. He packs his device away and buttons his cufflinks.

I've kept you for far too long, he says. Let me know when you have the package.

He adjusts his hat and somehow, his mask is already strapped over his face.

I'll be in touch, he says.

Then he nods and walks away from the three of us. He tips his hat at Nolwazi and finds the door.

We sit back on the couch, and I guess that's all there is between us.

It's happened.

The three of us are left alone in the yellow light and the

remaining ribbons of his cigarette smoke. Ruan, Cissie and I take a look around the empty bar. Then, with our beers turning to warm water between our knees, and almost at the same time, we whisper to each other, saying: what?

I get a delayed text message from my case manager, Sis' Thobeka. The three of us are back at Cissie's place, again, and Ruan's high on khat, playing an erratic set of drums on his kneecaps. We met a dealer in Rosebank who sold us twenty stems. He agreed to drop the price by a third.

At Cissie's place, we listen to Ruan as he drums. Pausing for a moment, he says we should just use the money and then kill ourselves.

That could be a life, he says.

Cissie and I agree. We share another stem and tell Ruan that this isn't a bad idea.

It's like that book, he says. There was a guy. He wrote a book and won a prize for it.

I open the text message and Sis' Thobeka says to me, Lindanathi, your CD4 count.

She writes: Lindanathi, you didn't fax us your CD4 sheet, I thought I told you yesterday to—

I delete her message.

Then Ruan says, I can't remember the guy who wrote that book. He tells us he's googling it and Cissie and I get up to watch. We lean over him, and, for the rest of the night, we keep stems between our teeth and chew until we can't feel our faces any more. Then we prod our fingers into each other's sides and laugh like well-fed children.

The following morning finds the three of us still awake. The sun rolls over Table Mountain just after six a.m. on Monday morning, and under it we lie sprawled across Cissie's leather sectional couch. It rained last night, and Cissie tells us there's a leak in the roof that's wet her cushion. She keeps extending a palm to pat the damp spot. Ruan and I lie still, watching her.

Guess what today is, she says.

What?

It's a holiday, Cissie sighs, but guess which one?

We can't, and when we don't answer her, she tells us it's Women's Day. I don't have to go in to work today and my aunt is still dead, she says. What now?

Ruan and I remain silent. Then Cissie falls back on the sectional couch and lies there, motionless.

Half an hour later, we shower and share what's left of the khat. Then we take the lift down to the ground floor and catch a taxi to the bottle store in Claremont, where we stock up on champagne and liqueurs and everything else we never drink. We walk out of the bottle store with a loaded shopping bag in each hand, skipping across the main road like the world might end tomorrow. Then I guess this is how we spend the rest of our Monday. We talk and sometimes the three of us shout, and then our vision grows sharp around four a.m. and we feel ourselves floating up to the ceiling, speaking many praises to each other's existence.

Sometime during the night, I think of my late brother. There were summers I'd take Luthando down the block in my old neighborhood, eMthatha, to a big white stippled house at the corner of Orchid and Aloe Streets, where an Afrikaans family from Bloemfontein had moved in. Their son, Werner, who was older than us by a few years, had taken control of his family's pool house; a flat at least twice the size of my room. Werner liked to make us watch him while he squeezed a tube of Dirkie condensed milk down his throat; and sometimes he'd command my brother and I to laugh with open mouths through his fart jokes, after which he'd collapse into a castle made from his bright plush toys. We always met Werner at the window of his room. He was an only child and coddled by both of his parents. Since moving into the neighborhood, his parents had banned him from leaving his yard; and LT and I had to jump their fence to register his presence. I suppose he was spoilt, in retrospect, almost to the point of seeming soft in the head. As a teen, his teeth had started to decay, turning brown in the center of his lower jaw, but he was also big-boned and well stocked, and would often bribe us over to his home with ice lollies and video games. I had my own video games by then, but not as many as Werner. My mother was still new at her government job and I couldn't show off in the way I wanted to about living in town. Lately, Luthando had started thinking he was better off than me. My brother had grown a patch of pubic hair the previous summer, and I wanted to remind him that he still ate sandwiches with pig fat at his house, and that one evening in Ngangelizwe, his mother had served us cups of samp water for supper.

Still, we hid together that day.

Like always, Werner told us his parents didn't allow Africans into their house. He called us blacks, to which we nodded, and then he threw the controllers through his burglar bars like bones on a leash. My brother and I scuttled after them on our bare and calloused feet. If Werner didn't win a game, he'd switch the console off and turn into an image of his father, barking us back onto the tar like a disgruntled *meneer* at the store, his face twisting as fierce as a boar's, fanning out a spray of saliva. When he did win, when Werner felt he'd won enough, he'd say his parents were due home in the next few minutes. Then he'd hoist the controllers back up and wipe them down with a wad of toilet paper. It was the same toilet paper he used to wipe semen off his plush toys, Luthando would later say to me.

He's a pig, your *bhulu* friend, he'd say, I've seen tissues of it all over his bedspread.

That day, Werner's parents came home early for a long

weekend and he hid us behind a sparse rosebush growing against their newly built fence. The day was gray, like most of them that summer, but the bricks in the wall were still warm. My brother and I were caught not thirty seconds later. Maybe Werner wanted us to be caught. The maid watched us with a blank mask from the kitchen sink while Werner's mother lost the blood in her face and his father, a large, balding architect with sleek black hair around a hard, shimmering pate, came after us with a roar, waving his belt over his head and shouting, *Uit! Uit! Uit!*

We were only twelve years old, so we ran.

Later, back home, Luthando found me in the kitchen and squeezed my nose between his thumbs from behind. We hadn't spoken since our escape from Werner's house, and I'd been making us coffee, watching as two of the neighborhood mutts mated lazily in the yard across from ours. My brother led me to a mirror and mashed my face into the cold pane. Luthando was in a rage, and he asked me if I liked looking that way—with my nose pinched—and nearly broke the glass with my forehead. I struggled and elbowed him and we both fell to the floor and fought. When he tired of pressing my face against the bathroom tile, and with my saliva pooling against my cheek on the floor, I asked him why he was hurting me, even though I knew the reason. Luthando said everything else about me was white, so why would I mind having a pinched nose on my face. Then he heeled my cheek again, and I thought it was to spite him that I smiled at what he'd said, but I knew even then a part of me was charmed by it. Eventually, when he got up and started to walk away, I tried to spit on his heels, and then I called him poor for the first time in our lives. This was me and my brother Luthando.

Masks, Ruan announces to us, dragging the word in a drawl through each syllable. Cissie and I watch him from the other side of her coffee table. We're inside the following day, just a minute after noon, and Ruan's voice sounds weak but determined.

Just because some people wear a mask, he says, that doesn't mean they've done something wrong.

Cissie and I nod.

Ruan sits across from us, printing out three paper masks for us to use.

It's been about forty-eight hours since we took the client's money, and now we're back at West Ridge Heights, again, watching as the sun slides itself past Cissie's living-room windows, throwing its rays across Cape Town's countless bricks and bonnets. With the weary ghosts of Newlands still keeping vigil in their comatose gardens—only now, according to Cissie, beginning to smell our wealth inside her cream-colored building— we pass around her kitchen scissors and knit together links of rubber bands, and then we pull our paper sheets over our faces and turn into people more important than we are. I guess this is what we're doing instead of discussing the client, and instead of discussing Sylvia, Cissie's aunt, whose body gets flown out in a pine box to Joburg today.

Cissie opens the biggest window in her living room and sighs. It's hot all over Cape Town today, she says.

I nod. You can feel the heat bouncing off the walls and sinking into the sectional couch, and when we get up and walk around the flat, we have everything off but our underwear. The way we drink, also, is by putting everything into Cissie's freezer: as soon as we've finished one bottle, we replace it with a full bottle of something else. We've left multicolored stains all over the kitchen floor.

In the living room, Ruan passes me another bottle of champagne and I take a deep swig. Then he stands up to tell us who he is today.

I guess this is how it sometimes starts with us. We have these games we waste our lives on just like everyone else, and today,

Ruan's up first and he tells us we should call him the country of Zimbabwe. The way he's standing in front of me and Cecelia, we're both sitting still on the leather sectional, and we're looking at the Robert Mugabe scowl pressed against his face. The gray printout hangs over his Adam's apple, a contrast to his wide, pale shoulders, and the way it's pulled back against his face, it looks like the beginning of a grimace, or like someone about to laugh. Then Ruan tells us he has thirteen million people inside of him, and lying down he's four hundred thousand square kilometers wide, and the way his pockets are set up, only seventy percent of his people live under the breadline.

In response, Cissie and I clap for him.

Then Cissie hands me the bottle of champagne and gets up from the couch in a white bra and boy shorts. She fixes Charles Taylor with rubber bands around her face, and tells us she's a hundred thousand square kilometers in size. Then she says she only has three million people living inside of her, and that the way her pockets are set up, only eighty percent of them live under the breadline. When Cissie's done, she drops herself next to me on the sectional couch, and I hand her the bottle of champagne.

Then I get up in front of them for my turn at the game.

I'm in my boxers, with a picture of Joseph Kabila on my face, and what I tell my friends is that overall, I'm two million square kilometers in size. I tell them that I've got sixty million people living inside of me, and the way my pockets are set up, only seventy percent of them live under my breadline. Then Cissie reaches over and I take the champagne from her and sit back down.

The three of us lie on the sofa and drink a while.

What if we had more money than any of the people in those countries? Cissie says. Or more money than their presidents.

Ruan lights a filter and shakes his head. I don't know about the presidents, he says.

Definitely not the presidents, I say. I get up for another bottle of champagne.

Then Cissie says, what if? She says, you know when people say the people? I always think presidents are what they mean when they say the people.

Explain, Ruan says.

I hand Cissie the bottle and she says, well, think about this. You remember about South Africa's first decade, right, from 1990? For years, South Africa was basically this one man. People used to call him *uTata we Sizwe*, the father of the nation.

I tell Cissie, sure. I remember this.

Then she says, that's around the same time we were born, right, as citizens? She says, so we all shared a father in that sense, didn't we?

Shared, Ruan says. What do you mean?

Cissie laughs. Okay, she says. I mean, sure, it's easy to dismiss the whole thing as some bullshit nationalism thing, isn't it? I get it, but that isn't my point. I think my point is more like, on a physical and cultural basis, we were all him, you know, we were all this one man from the island. Cissie asks if we understand her.

I tell her that I think I do. Or sometimes I think I do. Then I close my eyes and see myself back at the beach in Blouberg again. Falling back on the sectional couch, I watch as the ocean laps the quartz in the sand, the water rushing into Cissie's living room from every angle. From his side of the table, Ruan leans over his computer and his body divides into three bloodless sections. The light begins to intensify inside the living room, the Industrial flushing its final hum through my blood vessels, and I watch Cissie for a long time as she nods. Then I get up to get more champagne for the three of us, and when I return, Cissie says we should all get one big house. Sitting on the sectional couch, and with her head glowing like a child's crude drawing of the sun, with each light ray pushing out of her head in a thick, flat vector, she says to me, let's grow to be more than two million square kilometers in size. I nod and close my eyes against the glare, and for a long time, as I hear Cissie's voice expanding inside my head, the feeling I get, sitting here on her living-room floor, isn't about my uncle or Du Noon, it isn't about my sickness or my job. Instead, it's about the three of us sitting together in her flat in Newlands, the three of us knitting our fingers together, me, Ruan and Cecelia, closing our eyes and becoming one big house.

THIRD PART

NOW HERE I AM, SITTING WITH LUTHANDO, MY dead brother, and we're smoking cigarettes and drinking gin out of a tin can. The field in front of us keeps bursting into flames, but this is only happening inside my head, said our pastor, Mr. Pukwana, when my mother took me to him after service. When I blink, the fire disappears, and then Luthando says to me, Nathi, all you do is read books. I put the smoke out on the grass and say, my girlfriend said she hates violence. My brother ignores me. Her parents are rich, he says, why does she hate them so much? They aren't rich, I tell him. They just work for the homeland government. I tell Luthando I would hate them, too, if they were mine, and this makes him scoff. There's something wrong with you, Nathi, he says. I heard your mother say they're taking you to a doctor. I don't say anything back. The time right now is close to midnight, and we're at a park just a block from my house. Luthando takes out his *okapi* and, placing it flat against my neck, he says, let me kill you first. Then the world is black again, and my mind thrums like it does whenever I'm at my desk at school; whenever my eyes glide over the floor and I imagine meteoroids crashing through Mr. Peter's gabled roof. I breathe out smoke and cough until my eyes water. Then Luthando laughs and takes my notebook from me. I watch him running down the street. He shouts, why do you always make me so violent in your stories? Then he jumps into a cone of orange streetlight and, tapping his heels together like an actor from a musical, he says, I never killed anyone.

For a long time, I never thought about him, my dead brother. Luthando had passed away from us, had become another limb my family had to cut off and bury. I already knew how people could die. My grandmother's death had taught me that while I was still a junior in high school, and there'd also been the case of Bra Ishaak, just a few years before. We were only children when we first watched him fall on his face on a dry bed of paving gravel, his heels knocking together while he foamed a wild ribbon of saliva at the mouth. That was outside the Wendy flat at my grandmother's house, eQokolweni. He was an epileptic and the only Muslim in our family, an uncle I knew mostly from his ample and wet kisses, before my aunt—now also a skinless outline melting into the soil—found him hanging from the rafters of the chicken shed.

We wake up early and finish the rest of the champagne. Ruan prepares a tube of Industrial for us to use and we spend the next few hours weaving in and out of consciousness. It's a peaceful state: my thoughts meander over a dullness settled in my body. I can no longer tell what part of the day it is, or how long we've been sitting here at West Ridge Heights, waiting to hear from our client. Leaning back on the couch, I realize that my uncle has become a distant echo. I don't know where my cellphone is.

How many times do you think you've been inside a supermarket? Cissie says. I want you to answer me honestly. Think of this as your final Last Life question.

I don't know, I say. I used to have a job in one.

I remember this one afternoon when I still worked a till at the Spar in Rondebosch East. I'd taken a job there the previous summer, ringing up groceries and saving money for my first tubes of Industrial, and to supplement the rent for my new place in Obs. I only had three days a week, and nothing much had been happening that afternoon, a Thursday, except maybe for my walking away early from my shift.

We were in Ruan's living room, and Cissie was telling me that maybe he was right. This was the same Ruan who, with two cigarettes in his mouth, would tell you that every day the tobacco industry recruits three thousand new smokers to compensate for the ones it kills; the same Ruan who, without taking his eyes off his computer screen, would tell you that in some Asian country, seven hundred kids fell into a seizure after watching an animation program with bad lighting techniques.

He was now right.

Maybe my job is one of the most dangerous ones around, Cissie said, before sinking the bottleneck of beer between her lips.

The two of us were watching an old werewolf movie on mute. Cissie said she could stomach the gore, but it was really the screaming that got to her. Personally, I thought the silence was because she was trying to get closer to Zanele, her new deaf pupil at the daycare. Her job that she all of a sudden hated so much.

From somewhere upstairs, Ruan laughed. He was over downloading, he said, and had now taken to uploading parts of his soul to cyberspace.

In the lounge, Cissie took another sip.

Something else about her back then was that she always wore long-sleeved sweaters. Cissie had these bad rashes, and her arms gave her away as a human zebra with all that scar tissue. When she lifted her bottle, one of these scars looked at me, and she said, today, one of my kids swallowed a cup of detergent. Can you believe that? It had to be Zanele, of course. Joy and I had to call an ambulance out to Mowbray for her.

Then Cissie told me that Zanele's name meant that her parents had had enough girls.

Can you imagine that? she said.

I could, but the two of us didn't say much afterwards. We sat side by side for the rest of the afternoon, watching werewolves leap across courtyards in a foreign city. Later, when Ruan came downstairs, he was dressed in his boxers, a shirt and his ugly, badly made tie. He had his computer under one arm, its cords leading all the way to the room upstairs; and standing at the foot of the staircase, he told us, salvation.

Cissie drank her beer and Ruan asked me to imagine my entire being reduced to the size of an electron, living free in the vastness of cyberspace.

I decided to let my friends in on a bit more detail about myself. I told them that, apart from being numbed daily from the waist down by spending eight hours packing people's groceries, I also committed genocidal murder. I told them it didn't matter what they looked like or who they were, whether they greeted or not. I killed them without accounting for difference.

Cissie remained silent. Ruan typed on his computer and swiveled the screen so I could read it. It said, make the choice to transmute: discard all desire for a better prison.

Then Cissie finished her beer and reached for mine on the coffee table. She nodded and told me to go on.

I did. I told them that once, this lady had forgotten that I'd given her her change. She'd had an outburst at my station, and in response I'd stuffed her baby's leg down her throat. This was my third hour at work, I said, and I had twenty-five casualties and counting.

On the TV screen the credits for the werewolf movie rolled, revealing true identities as they emerged from the horizon of a nightmare, and Ruan typed on his computer again. He swivelled the screen and this time it said, forgo the desire for permanence: locate the ending in all experience.

For a while, Cissie and I listened to the patter of his keyboard. Then I told them I couldn't live like that anymore. I told them there was only one way to end it and Cissie looked at me through an empty beer bottle and asked me how; and that's when I told her I was the next casualty.

Once, Ruan says to us now, in Cissie's living room, and Cissie and I both nod. It's a good answer, I tell him, and he grins before he starts to yawn.

Once, he says, because he hasn't found an exit, yet.

Cissie and I agree.

Maybe we were never meant to, Cissie says.

In response, Ruan shrugs. Then Cissie gets up to switch on her TV. It's this old black and white unit, and Ruan and I sit back, watching her as she flips through its channels.

Part of the appeal of television, Ruan says, is that it arrived to our marketplace with a limited range for choice. It was possible to feel absolved in taking in its misinformation, he says, because the communication was always one-sided.

On the TV screen now, advertisements roll out the reverse images of people who smile back at us, while exploding angelic-chorus slogans narrate their thirty-second lives into acne cream, nationalism, and McDonald's.

In between, Cissie changes the channel and it's the parliament broadcast.

In between, Cissie changes the channel and it's the Christian network.

I rub my eyes and lean back.

I believe insanity is a different way of thinking caused by exposure to pollution as a child, Ruan says. Then he looks up at the TV and back at me.

He says, I know what you're thinking.

What?

That the Americans didn't land on the moon. That the "Star-Spangled Banner" is stuck atop the tower of Babel.

I don't say anything to him. I lay my head on the sofa and close my eyes.

In the spring of 1979, Ruan says, an Israeli atomic bomb was detonated a thousand kilometers off the coast of Cape Town, and not long after that, a satellite detected the double flash between the Prince Edward and Crozet Islands. Later, the Israeli government denied the existence of the explosion and attributed the flash to a fault in the satellite's mapping system, and maybe, Ruan says to us, this means we've all lived through a nuclear apocalypse.

Listening to him, I think of the ocean, again. The first time I heard of the open sea was when my uncle squeezed my head between his palms and lifted me up to get a view of the shoreline from my grandmother's village, which I never saw, but succeeded in instilling in me the idea that the natural world was without borders.

Later, after a day of stoning crabs and using the clay on the river bank to mold sculptures of my grandmother's cattle, Bra Ishaak cautioned us against killing living creatures for sport, warning us that at night we would be visited by the forebears of these crabs, who would knock on our doors with bodies as tall as men.

Maybe they were Ruan's survivors, too.

Lying on the sofa, I open my eyes again and wait for them to regain their focus.

Then Cissie turns off the TV.

The three of us take more khat. The hours start slipping over and through us again, and two days later, when a humid Thursday settles over Newlands, we receive a phone call from our client. He tells Ruan to put his voice on the loud speaker.

Cissie fills a milk jug with ginger-flavored ice blocks and places it on the table top. Then the three of us edge in closer to listen.

When Bra Ishaak hung himself, it was also a Thursday morning, back east in Uitenhage; he wore a sailor's hat on the day he finally chose to leave us, his family, behind. People died, I decided then. I said it again years later at LT's funeral, when the rain clouds dropped and smoked up the hillside that nursed his grave like an open wound, the mist moistening our necks and beading our sunglasses under the gray light. I said that people die. Then I cupped dirt over his door-shaped hole and picked up the shovel they gave us to bury him.

The old-timers were the first to thread away from us, most of them silenced altogether by the business of Luthando's death. LT was one of three recent casualties in our village, and our elders had grown concerned over this peak in numbers. Death wasn't new to the camps, but this was still a decade before as many as thirty boys could fall in a season. They knew that Luthando had stolen into a neighbor's ceremony, and that he hadn't been assigned a surgeon of his own, but that there were many boys who'd won the community's admiration for stealing into camps. It was a sport for many. Even before the legislature had reached into our village, our surgeons had seldom shared their blades between initiates. There was the mixing of blood to contend with, but it was also a point of pride for a family to hire a man with a name. No anesthetic was used on the wound, and the blood had to be stopped by palming a clutch of herbs on the cut. It needed someone quick with their hands, and with his mind set on the work, before *ukhanki*, the healer, would walk into a hut with less care and less pay. Our elders had always been wary of giving too much room to questions posed against their customs, but now, sitting in silence as Sis' Funeka spoke of my brother from a raised platform, having to be helped back to her feet when she collapsed towards the end, they knew they'd have to reconsider their stance. That day, they folded their hats throughout the sermon, and pressed snuff up their noses on their way out after bending over to wash their hands free of Luthando's spirit, *emadlakeni*, in a cracked white bucket.

Maybe I didn't wash my hands free of my little brother at that gate. I can't remember if I knelt for him or not.

Over the line, before receiving his first order, our client places another. Then he slots in a meeting with us on the following Sunday. Through the speaker, his voice has a lot of verve, and his tone is louder than it sounded in the bar. Ruan, Cissie and I listen to his terms. Intimidated, we agree to sell him everything he wants. From the beginning, he expresses an interest in our next two packages.

When he puts the phone down, we sit and try to think of something else, but nothing comes. Instead, we take more khat and watch the rest of the week passing over us, most of it feeling like a single day. Later, when I ask Cissie and Ruan about this, the two of them confess to having felt the same way.

On Sunday, we take the train out to see him.

We've run out of painkillers, Ruan says, sounding mournful as we get our tickets stubbed at the platform in Obs. We still have our money, but we've grown hesitant about spending more of it. We haven't delivered the ARVs to the client yet, and the deposit still belongs on his side of the transaction.

I get paid soon, Cissie offers, and we decide to leave it at that. Then the train moves on, grinding down on its rails, and we carry our comedowns with us across Salt River.

We get off in Woodstock on an empty platform and find our way out of the station. The client's given us directions, instructing us to climb up Mountain Road and then take the second turn on the right; and so we do that. As we walk up, the sun bears down through the clear sky, and the city feels half asleep once more, with only two taxis moving along the unending stretch of the main road.

The following morning, at the supermarket, and on a Friday in which nothing much happened, except maybe for my being early for my shift, a woman with dark hair and a red face approached my till, slammed a serrated knife on my counter and began to shout. She showed me how the wooden handle was missing screws and some of her saliva sprayed on my face as she asked me what type of place I was running there. I'd never run anything in my life, I thought, but I took the knife anyway.

Please ma'am, I said, let me go fetch you another utensil. I'll take this up with the manager, I offered, which only made her look away in disgust.

I took the knife, closed my eyes, opened them and started walking. I walked past her and into the full light of the fluorescents. I walked towards the aisle where the knives were. I walked past it, and then I walked past the manager's office, too. The knife's packaging, which was hard plastic, was sticking to my palm. When I placed my free hand on the door handle of the rest room, Jill, a fellow employee, called out to me. She asked me what I was up to, so I told her I was pleasing a customer. Then I smiled.

I swear, Jill said, the way these people are so inconsiderate, they could drive someone to suicide. Jill had green eyes and a long fringe she liked to blow off her face. She always stood with one hand on her waist—either at the parcel check or the kiosk—her paunch pushed forward at an angle from her small frame.

I nodded. Then I stepped into the rest room, but, before I closed the door I turned to face her, and when the frame broke the fluorescent light into dark drawn-out shadows on my face, like I'd seen it do with any number of us when we stood there, my smile widened and I said to her, tell me about it. Then I sat there for a long time before I took the knife back to the storeroom.

We arrive at a small house on the corner of Milner and Lawley Streets. The door's blue, and it hangs in front of us, under a dimpled pane. Its peeling panels look close to ruin, and it stands just a meter behind a white fence. When I knock, there's no answer, and Cissie asks me if we've arrived at the right place. She edges up towards me and I knock again, but still no one replies.

Eventually, I turn around and look up the road. On the opposite side, I see two teenage girls lounging on the back seat of a gold Cressida, their legs hanging out of the windows. In the sunlight, their thighs look as thin as arms, and I can hear the murmur of their voices hissing under the silence. A man with short dreadlocks, wearing a navy soccer shirt, pushes a trolley down the road towards us. He has his boots hanging around his neck by thick red laces, and he stumbles as he steers the trolley over the pavement. Occasionally, he shakes his head and shouts into the cage. When at last he pushes past the three of us, I turn to Cissie and Ruan and tell them I have a feeling we've arrived at the right place.

You sure?

I'm not.

I guess none of us are, Cissie says, and puts out her cigarette.

I turn back to the door and push it as hard as I can, and it clicks open when I give it a third shove. Ruan, Cissie and I file in, making our way into a small foyer.

Inside, the building feels cramped, despite its emptiness, and smells coated with an old layer of dust. We take measured steps, our feet falling in a soft pattern over the carpet. The client isn't anywhere in sight, but his voice seems to carry from every room in the house. Maybe it's in my head, but I can feel it shaking the walls. Then the front door slams closed behind us and we stop moving. His voice beckons us closer. Then he starts laughing. Ruan, Cissie and I walk towards him, one after the other.

We don't find him waiting in the living room, and we don't find him waiting in the kitchen, either, or even in the bathroom. Instead, we find his voice speaking to us without the presence of his body. There's a laptop, with a camera fitted over the screen, balanced against a green vase on a coffee table. The three of us take our seats on a sofa in front of it. The man's silhouette is spread out on the display. The audio jack's connected to a stereo system set up on the tiled floor in the corner, and it pushes his voice into the house. Ruan, Cissie and I sit in silence.

We wait for the man to start. I look through the curtain lace and notice the glimmer of the gold Cressida again. It makes its way down Lawley Street, the legs of the girls still hanging out of its back-seat windows.

Then the man shuffles to life inside the screen's frame. His silhouette moves, and he tells us that he's prepared a game for us to play.

We listen.

It will be my very last game, he says.

We watch him light a cigarette. He takes a slow drag through the tube in his neck, then lets the smoke funnel back out in a thin plume. It curls at the top of his screen, crowning him with a small firmament. Then he starts to whistle, and in the middle of the frame, his face takes on the form of a dark landscape, rolling unevenly below a blue mist.

Once, he says to us—and Ruan, Cissie, and I draw in, pitching our heads forward to listen—there was a small and hidden village. It wasn't very far from this city where the four of us now take our seats, holding our palaver across this wire. It was small, and known only to its inhabitants. They had no ruler, and had seen it fit to name their village after the harvest bounty, a word in a dialect now disappeared from this world. One year, the rains held off, and in the following seasons, the land was struck by a heat wave—the beginning of blight and famine. Then one day, the elders instructed the children in the village to go searching for quarry and crops, and when they returned, sorrowful and without reward, they all fell into a deep sleep. The following morning, the children began to grow roots on their scalps, and within a fortnight they had banana saplings growing out of their heads. The elders, famished, took only a day to deliberate. Then they decided to dig early graves for the children so the saplings might grow into trees. There would be more children, they reasoned. Then they buried them. They watered the graves with their tears and the saplings grew into trees and they feasted. However, soon after the elders had taken their fill, they fell into a deep slumber and awoke to find roots growing out of their own heads. The bark from the saplings thickened and pushed down on their weak joints, and within a day they were buried below the earth. Later that same evening, the sky opened itself with a thunderclap, and now a grove of banana trees stands where those villagers once lived. Do you understand me?

I do.

This comes from Cecelia. She says it without hesitation and lifts herself up from the couch. Surprised, Ruan and I turn to face her.

Good, the man replies. He lights another cigarette and draws the smoke slowly through the tube. Then he motions his hand towards a door on the left side of the hallway. The three of us follow his gesture with our eyes. You'll find more inside, he says, and Cissie nods.

In silence, she walks across the hallway and enters the room to the left. The door closes behind her and the ugly man continues.

Once, he says again, there was a man who was a carpenter and a spirit man.

The man exhales the smoke through his nose and continues.

Since the carpenter was blessed with both craftiness and piety, he says, with firm fingers that carried the land's wisdoms as well as a porous spirit, he was valued widely across the region. However, he had been born with a nose that was moved too far to the left of his face, and a cleft palate, disfigurements which delivered him daily into the clutches of shame. He was unable to bear the company of his neighbors, and, as a result, lived the life of a fugitive. In each village he passed, he was seen only as a faint figure on the hills, where he would set up his hut far from the eyes of the villagers below. One night, alone in such a hut, his ears growing heavy with the cheers of a harvest festival below, a notion came to him. He would fashion a wooden sculpture in his own image, only amending it where the disfigurements had struck his face. He labored for two days without rest, and was done as the third day dawned, upon which he beheld his work. The following day, he smuggled the sculpture to the village below, where it was received with praise and admiration. However, when he descended from his mountain to meet the villagers and reveal himself as its creator, no one recognized him. Instead, he was captured and then banished for vagrancy. Do you understand me?

I watch Ruan as he raises his head and looks at the screen. He nods.

The man tells him to look to the door on the right. He motions with his hand and tells him to go inside.

Ruan sighs. Then he lifts himself off the sofa and disappears into the right wall.

I wait.

Inside the computer, the man allows the smoke to seep out through his nostrils. This is for you, Lindanathi, he says, and I listen.

Once, a canopy of plants grew to cover the sky over a great city. For as far as one could see, the land had grown into a rainforest, a second set of lungs for planet Earth. Rejoicing, the people took cover under its shade, surrounding themselves with the plenitude of its fruit. For years, the people fed and took shelter under the canopy. Then there was something else. The forest demanded more room. The middle classes were hung up by their ankles from the high weave of branches. Then the prison warders, together with police captains and constables, uncaged members of the prison gangs, spilling armies of these men into the city's streets. In the end, the authorities pitted the gangsters against each other in circle fights, while members of the middle class, in the fashion of rotted plantains, snapped off the branches and dropped into the center of the maul. Do you understand?

I nod.

I don't recall getting to my feet, but I find myself standing.

In front of me, the screen begins to blink.

Then the man's voice booms out from the walls again, and he tells me to walk towards the room at the end of the hallway.

I walk.

Inside the room, there's no light, but I can make out a bed. Feeling dizzy, I grope for it in the dark.

Then I lie down on the single mattress, thinking of Ruan and Cecelia. My eyelids start to weigh down on my eyes, and my breath leaves me as if for the final time.

Cecelia

The first time I thought about dying—thought about it at length, the way I do now—goes so far back I get a headache whenever Ruan and Nathi ask me about it. The two of them know it's an old story, but they still bother me about what happened that night.

Well, it started with me and my friend Claire.

I'd got to know Claire over the internet the previous summer. We'd met by chance, in a chat room about Rothko, an artist we were both trying to emulate at the time. I knew from the beginning that Claire was an exceptional painter, the kind of artist a Pretoria high school student wouldn't usually get to know. I considered myself lucky. Claire wasn't a famous artist; she wasn't in coffee-table books or hung at the Fried Contemporary, but she was timely and transparent. Or at least she was those things to me. I was sixteen. It had been four years since my mother died and I was living with my aunt, Sylvia, in a townhouse in Mooikloof. Claire had just turned twenty-eight.

We'd chat for hours, most days, until late in the evening. Everyone thought Claire should be in a hospital, she told me, and sometimes she'd say she was texting me from one, a psychiatric clinic in Grahamstown or in Randburg, but I wasn't always sure I believed her. Later, I decided there was a lot my friend was putting on for me—that Claire could be more than a little pretentious—but I also knew that I liked that about her. I wanted us to keep in touch, so I sent her emails and jokes whenever she told me she'd been admitted.

We talked about the death thing a few months in. One night, in a long email, Claire told me about her mother. She said that once, when nobody was looking and everyone was thinking Claire was so brave for not crying, she tried to pull her mother off a life-support machine. She told me how she didn't think, how she just reached for the plug and pulled. On the hospital bed, with all those tubes and needles and vials, her mother kept her eyes closed and hid a smile underneath her oxygen mask.

Claire told me that her mother, a self-taught water-color artist and an anthropologist at Rhodes, really liked to suffer, and that she pulled this guilt-trip shit on everyone she met. Claire told me to imagine being like that—hurting myself so I could suffer with the rest of the planet. It's all very artistic and exhausting, she said.

Then she asked me about what happened with my mother, and I told her. I said I did what she'd tried to do. I pulled my mother off life-support. Only I didn't use a plug. It was me that I removed from the side of her bed: when my mother's stomach cancer got serious, I began to keep away from the hospital. When she requested to see me, I pretended to agree, but never showed up at the ward. Maybe I wanted to preserve her, I said to Claire. This was how my mother had stayed alive in my head for so long after she was gone.

Ruan

The last job I had, before my uncle took me in, was a post as a high school sport medic. I was twenty-two, and, for a while, I made enough to get by. Most days, I'd be at some high school holding an ice pack to a kid's nose. There'd be blood flowing down the length of my arm and this kid, he'd say I'm wasting his time. He'd tell me to let him go. He'd tell me, I'm fine, I'm fine, Jesus. It's not like I've never had a nosebleed before.

Those days, a guy called Ralph used to supervise me. From the side of the field, he'd motion with his arms and tell me what to do.

Usually: Ruan, what the fuck are you doing?

Usually: Let the kid play, for Christ's sake.

On most days, before he became my supervisor, Ralph was a gambler. He liked to tell me I was losing him money when I did my job. We had a lot of guys like that. Guys who believed the AIDS-infected should be put on one island and left to fend for themselves; guys who laughed and joked about how every chip you ate was another Ethiopian family dead.

I often saw myself back at my flat. Inside my shower, I would add more grime to the grout between the tiles. I would wash what was left of the blood from my armpits.

Sometimes I asked myself, you eat with these same hands?

I asked myself, what are you doing here?

Then I met Part.

When the two of us got together, I told her it's funny about my being ugly, because when God was making faces, I wasn't by his side telling him to give me eyes like a movie star.

We were inside my van, where it felt like we were inside a womb, incubating. The noise outside was a hum while Part, with her short skirt and hands on her knees, asked me how bad the bleeding got from an overdose of pethidine.

Her question didn't surprise me. Teenage girls tried to score drugs from me all the time, and some people thought that was my job. The truth was, our strongest drugs were headache tablets, and mostly we just reserved gauze swabs and vials of iodine.

Still, I smiled at her, in that funny way I have.

I told her the uglier I look on the outside, the more of the opposite I am on the inside.

I'm not really hurt, she said, before shooting up with an imaginary needle. Something I'd noticed about her was that her hair was symmetrical. When she raised her arm to shoot up again, her legs parted a bit wider, and her panties reflected on the stretcher's silver bar.

You know, she said, my father works for the police, and he says the first thing you do when you question someone is to look at their facial bone structure.

I nodded.

She told me that if you're self-conscious, you don't believe in yourself, let alone your lies, and that in history, the saints were just people who got through their self-loathing by praising someone else.

I nodded again, and this made her draw closer.

Part told me she was eighteen. She was the only person I'd get to know before I met Nathi and Cecelia.

That day, her panties slid down her waist while her skirt hitched upwards. Inside my van, I imagined that the time I could spend in jail for being together with her was the time it had taken me to accept that these afternoons on the fields were adding up to my life. The way Part and I came together; that afternoon, in between kisses, she told me repeatedly how fucked I was, she told me repeatedly how my face meant I would never be able to lie.

Me

Cissie and I sometimes go to the cemetery, where we test the ground and tell each other to choose sites. My friend Cecelia, the smart one, the artist, she's the reason for this, and she tells me we're preparing ourselves for the end of the world. Today, she's all orange flowing hair and marijuana. She squints at the sunset bleeding behind the hills and tells me, when it comes, it won't be mass destruction; the end of the world is the destruction of the individual.

Cissie says she was friends with a famous artist in high school. Myself, back then, I was anyone I could find.

Exhaling, I say, subjectivity causes a switch between existence and the individual.

Cissie looks at me and I knit my fingers, letting the sun's blood seep in between. For a long time, I could never look at her. Cecelia, the agonizing artist; Cecelia, the cliché. I always looked at her when she wasn't looking at me. That way, I wouldn't fall for her for being beautiful and she wouldn't pity me for being sick.

We often choose the old cemetery in Rondebosch, opposite the mall and the restaurants.

Cissie sinks her fingers into the soil and brings up blades of grass between black fingernails. Then she brings her other hand down and puts the joint out on the bare patch. Sorry, Mom, she says.

Later, I can't sleep and have to do the next best thing and pass out. We've cleaned out the liquor stash and the glue, so I head straight for the fridge and look for the champagne. I miss my grandmother in a way that makes me feel sick again, and I watch another movie that convinces me I have AIDS. There's a quarter of the champagne left and the bubbles have gone flat. I only have HIV, I say, I don't have AIDS, and when I take a swig from the bottle, the champagne tastes like lemonade inside my mouth.

We wake up early the following morning, and it takes me a while to orientate myself, to remember that we're still in Woodstock, divided by the narrow hallway. The electric buzz from the stereo system thrums hard against the walls, and I can feel it pushing a thick hum against the window panes. I sit up on the single mattress and notice the number 718 written in red marker across the wall. The springs creak beneath me. I don't know what to make of it, so I get up and rub my palms against my eyes.

Stepping out of my room, I find Cissie and Ruan doing the same across the hall. For a while, the three of us stand groggily at our thresholds. Then we shuffle together into the living room. On the coffee table, the laptop has disappeared. In its place, lying in front of the green vase, there's an envelope addressed to the three of us.

We take a seat on the sofa.

Then Cissie opens the letter.

Friends, it reads.

It's written in green ink, in neat block letters. Further down it says, before I thank you, please allow me to request your numbers from you.

Ruan, Cissie, and I look up. Then we turn and walk to our bedrooms. Moving like automatons, the three of us come back to the living room and settle on the couch, each choosing the same cushion as before. Our forearms rub against each other's, as cold as they were on Julian's balcony. There's a pen on the tabletop, and I use it to write down 718 in the space left open under the green script. Then Cissie writes down 817, and Ruan 178.

We read on. The letter says, turn me around, and so we do that. We turn the page over. On the back there's an explanation. It isn't too long.

The client says he didn't use any drugs on us, just hypnosis. He says we looked like we needed the rest.

Then he tells us about the numbers, how they're a code to a safety deposit box. He'd like us to deliver the contents of the box to someone he can no longer visit.

I look up and, sitting here in the client's empty house in Woodstock, on the corner of Milner and Lawley Streets, and with the world outside muted as the morning light pushes itself against the panes, I wonder why he'd ask us to do this for him. Ruan, Cissie and me, with our pill operation and our need for money. Then it comes to me that this is what he wanted from us all along. Once this idea announces itself, it refuses to take leave of me.

For a moment, the three of us are silent, and then we read on.

I asked my daughter, the ugly man writes, who told me you were the only adults that she knew.

I pause.

Then I look up again, and that's when I see it: lying flat on the table behind the vase is a photograph of Ethelia, now without her secret empires in West Ridge.

When I got stabbed in Obs, I was told to wait before the ambulance arrived, and I waited. Then I heard my blood filling up in my ears and I began to walk. They found me on Station Road, my blood leaking off a light pole. It was an important occasion, I thought, when the paramedics finally arrived. They got away with all my belongings, I told them, watching as the medics crouched to pull me up by my armpits. I had a cellphone and a bank card, I explained, and the two of them nodded, but didn't speak to me.

Luthando also saved my life, once.

My brother and I were visiting at our cousins' house that summer, and one Saturday we made a go-kart. When I took it for a test run, with Luthando running beside me, I jerked the steering wheel, but the wheels wouldn't turn. Before I slid into the traffic, Luthando clutched my wrist and pulled me off the wood. The go-kart flipped over on its side, and from between my knees I watched as the cars missed my feet by a few inches. The axle wasn't working, we figured. Then Luthando and I pulled the kart back up and dragged it home. It's rotten, he said, breaking its wheels in the silence that followed. Then we ran to the playing fields that blocked off Bisho Park—which lay to the north of our grand-aunt's house; an unsafe area, my mother had told me—where we stalked merry-go-rounds and chafed big blisters on our thighs by going on the metal slide in shorts. On Saturdays, after bowls of porridge we soured with vinegar—or thickened with scoops of peanut butter or margarine—Luthando and I flipped a fifty-cent coin to decide who would push and who would ride; and then we'd pump our calves stiff on the creaking swings at the park, pulling their chains taut as we swung for reputation and bragging rights against the neighborhood kids.

The paramedics got me up and strapped me to a gurney. That's when I thought of that go-kart we'd had.

The three of us drove in silence through the suburb where my pockets had been emptied. We went over the bridge, across Lower Main Road and up to Groote Schuur Hospital, where I felt the air change. The paramedics gave me a bandage to press on my wound and I was told to wait until I received assistance. Then a nurse arrived and took me to a bright room where there were more of us in the middle of dying. I was given a seat next to a large-eared man who sat reading the paper. My neighbor glanced at me for a moment before he leaned his head back to sleep. I watched him press the loose pages of the *Cape Times* into a tent over his face. The wheels of another gurney creaked behind us. This one carried a teenager—a boy from Beacon Valley, the medics said—who'd been shot in both legs. He was around sixteen, and was wheeled into the ward unconscious. The bandages around his thighs were dark with blood, the cloth rough from the bone splintered beneath.

I began to lose consciousness in my seat. Then I heard them call my name. Two more nurses arrived to help me up and I was passed through a door and sat in front of a doctor. The doctor was a balding, middle-aged man with spectacles pushed up his forehead. He instructed me from behind his desk, and I peeled off my clothes and showed him my injuries. He used a needle to anesthetize the nerve endings around the wound, and then he used another with a thread to sew it shut. I felt a hot flush before my skin receded back into numbness. Then I was led out and given a bed by a window. They discharged me the following day, on a Sunday morning, and I received my bill a month later.

On the eighth of August, two and a half months after I was stabbed and robbed in Observatory, I resigned from my lab-assistant post in the molecular biology department. My job had been to test samples for HIV antibodies. Those that came out reactive—testing positive for the virus—we divided into HIV-1 and HIV-2. The samples that came back negative we sent for further tests, hoping to detect a genetic mutation that gave a small percentage of the population immunity. Towards the conclusion of this project, which had lasted three years, I scheduled a meeting with the director to finalize the terms of my resignation: the size of my severance pay and the retirement fund I'd take home.

My boss at Peninsula Tech was a Frenchman. We all liked to refer to him as Le Roi, to tease him for his *noblesse oblige*. His real name was André. In his own eyes, philanthropy was the foremost principle of his work as a scientist, and one he encouraged in all the projects we saw coming in and out of the department. Often, Le Roi lightheartedly mocked himself for living a life without trouble in Africa, a continent he characterized by its health and economic crises; and even though I laughed along to his particular brand of wit, which I found quick, it wasn't unreasonable to assume that he felt just as sorry for me—that I was, after all, just another of his Africans.

Still, I didn't make too much of it.

Look, I'm very sorry to lose you, André told me after he summoned me into his office, but why not take some time off? You've had an ordeal, you need some rest, he said.

He struggled to keep his eyes on me as he spoke.

Le Roi told me I could sit on my arse at home if I wanted to. For a while, at least. I mean, come on, he said, you deserve it.

I understood his method. It was important for people in our profession to maintain a casualness around the virus. Even back then, we had to apply reins on how we expressed ourselves on the issue. There was the stigma to bargain with. Even in the most controlled cases, when mishandled, empathy could register as a cause for despair in a patient.

I watched Le Roi settle his eyes on his hands. The two of us fell silent for a while.

It's not the department's fault, I told him.

He nodded. I could tell he was pensive, but receptive.

If anyone's, I continued, it's my own.

Le Roi shook his head. Then he threw his hands up and said, who bloody well cares? Look, you're still a boy. You're a baby. You have a long life ahead of you.

I nodded.

I thought, what else can I do?

Then Le Roi clicked his fingers. The two of us were seated on his leather swivel chairs. He spun his eyes around in his head and grinned over the feel of his new leather blotter. It was engraved with his initials, he told me, before pointing out each letter. He'd had it shipped in that morning, and as he caressed it with his palms, he said something about his wife and a connection. Leaning across his desk, he gave me a reference letter in an envelope.

Of course, everything else will be taken care of, he said.

I nodded.

Then my boss sat on his side of the table and looked down at his blotter. I imagined Le Roi thinking of my accident as much as I was. I couldn't think of anything else we could have in common. Then I got up and left his office with my envelope.

It was gray and anemic outside. I found a sandwich bar on a corner of Long Street, where a customer had abandoned a book of T.S. Eliot poems on a low table. Sitting with the envelope still unopened in my jacket, I looked at the many lines the poet had hunched over between 1909 and 1962, and then at the coffee table itself, where my tumbler and tea pot sat empty. For a while, I listened to the rain clattering against the roofs of the cars parked outside. Then I put the book down and rubbed the motes out of my eyes. The couch beneath me was made of leather and was comfortable, and I craned my neck to see how the weather had turned outside. The rain had thickened and was bulleting down between the buildings of the City Bowl, punishing the bonnets of German sports cars and the canopies of pita-delivery vans. In the gutter, it raised a soft mist that curled like theatrical fog above the tar, and I saw couples rushing hand in hand to crowd together under the canvas awnings of the bars and the cafés, the teenagers in their school uniforms, the university students with their shopping bags lifted high over their heads. In the sky above them stood the city's many scaffolds, each rising like the skeleton of a grand and incomplete beast, abandoned by the calloused hands which were meant to bring it into existence.

I took a breath. Then I dug out the envelope.

With the reference letter, there was a small note with an email address written on it. To supplement my severance pay, Le Roi suggested I try my hand at freelance writing. It was something I could do with my time, he advised, but a strange idea to push on a techie like me, I thought. He must've seen me sitting down with a book when I brought my sandwiches into the labs sometimes, or maybe reading on the terrace that faced the campus square, where we had the habit of taking our cigarettes in our white lab-coats, struggling to conceal our envy for the leisure of the first- and second-year students.

This was how I went to work. I had enough books to hide my face behind during shifts. My colleagues were much older and we had very little in common outside the job.

I was alone for most of the time: taking down a tube of Industrial each week and longing to control my student debt, which I monitored on my laptop each night. Some days, I couldn't put anything in order. Often, I went home with a bottle of wine and watched the sun sliding past the Earth's waist, sitting back on my plastic chair on the balcony. I'd wait for the sun to go down, and only go back inside when I was certain I was feeling cold.

I lived in a flat opposite a small bar in Mowbray, and each night I'd watch it open its doors to the street. Its patrons were mostly commuters, men in blue overalls and black petrol-logo caps, but it also drew in the local prostitutes and a handful of students, all of whom it would slosh between its wooden teeth and gums for hours on end, waiting for the first signs of morning before it allowed them to totter out of its warmth, jubilant or groaning.

My colleagues, on the other hand, had families. They had satellite TV and good skin that could flush red with gratitude. They were well adjusted and easy to admire. Even those who came from places redolent of defeat—District Six, Bo-Kaap or

Bonteheuwel—were happy with what they had. I often felt scrutinized by them, and inadequate when we cornered each other in the hallways. Nothing was lost in the silence of our elevator rides. I'd greet my co-workers with a grin, feeling myself expand with the need to rush after them and apologize for something I hadn't done. Owing to this, I got my library card only a few months into the job.

In short, Le Roi had located something in me I couldn't deny.

The waitress arrived to tidy up my table. The rain had softened into a sparse tapping on the bonnets of the cars parked outside, and she asked me if I wanted more tea. I shook my head.

Outside, the cars weaved around the corners of the city grid. I felt wrapped in two skins as I pushed up against the wind. *The giving famishes the craving*, T.S. Eliot wrote. Now I stood on the corner of Long and Strand. I understand none of it, I thought, as I entered an empty taxi. I paid the *gaartjie* five rand and we headed down to Adderley Street, and when I looked up, storm clouds had started to wad themselves against the sun like gunpowder.

Then night time came.
Then daytime.
Then night time again.
Then daytime.
It went on like this for a while.

The first few days without work passed without ease. I cleaned and arranged the things I owned in my flat. I wound up taking an inventory of them from where I was lying on my bed, gauging the material rewards I'd accrued from my labor at the college. Then I used Handy Andy around my hotplate and mopped up the bathroom floor. I wiped off every insect I found on the window pane, and slowly began to adjust to not having a schedule. I decided to cut down on my use of Industrial, sticking to half a fingernail each day, which would thin my usage to only two-and-a-half tubes a month.

I waited one more week before I took out Le Roi's note. Then I sent off a copy of my CV to the email address he'd given me. I'd attached it to a cover letter with two paragraphs of tepid motivation. In under a week's time, I received my first response. I'd been solicited to write something right away. The company was a new website portal that catered to a wide variety of markets, ranging from celebrity gossip to women's health. It was part of the oldest media group in the country, not without its own checkered past, and, despite Le Roi's many apologies to Africa, his wife now owned a portion of it. My job was to write for the health segment of the portal. I had to use my knowledge of working in a sterile laboratory environment to give advice on avoiding germs in the workplace.

The company had been forward thinking. This was still a few years before the outbreak of SARS, the respiratory disease that would tide across the world's news portals from November 2002, when a furtive market was finally discovered among the hypochondriacs and health hobbyists. I had the prototype of this market as my readership.

My articles were only three- to eight-hundred-word pieces, limited to basic hygiene principles and the prevention of infection, so they weren't taxing for me to write. My first batch was received so well I couldn't help but suspect that Le Roi, in his pity for me, had greased the commissioning editor.

Not that I would argue if he had.

I drafted an invoice, despite these thoughts, and got on with writing more pieces. Then, before I knew it, a few months had passed and I was invited to join the permanent staff. I moved into a new office in Green Point, and soon after that I received my first compensation pay from the technikon. I used it to find a medical-aid scheme for my illness. That was how I met Sis' Thobeka, my case manager, and started my anti-retroviral treatment.

In the end, however, I couldn't tell if my articles drew anyone to the website portal, or if they'd been helpful in any way to the people that read them. That same summer, just before the end of December, the company reported a drop in its turnover, they announced a need to restructure, and half of us were dismissed.

The cause, as explained to us by the editor, was anyone's guess. The directors led us in a brief discussion about the slow growth of the digital economy, explaining why redundancies were inevitable across the board. They played us a succession of PowerPoint slides, demonstrating the numbers, but most of us couldn't imagine the sums they mentioned.

In the dark, I began to feel as if this crisis meeting, in which my colleagues and I sat mostly silent, was something that had taken place before. This sense of déjà vu would only fade months later, when I saw that the restructure they'd had in mind included disposing of half the human staff, and that the content was now collected from different sources across the Net. I realized then that the feeling I'd had at the meeting had arisen from the fact that, even as we'd sat in the ninth-floor boardroom that day, we'd formed part of a historical moment that had receded. Much like light traveling from the sun, although it had seemed immediate, it had taken time to reach us: the event itself had already taken place. We were obsolete.

Margeaux, who'd been the head of our editorial team just a moment earlier, suggested we meet up afterwards, breaking the silence that had fallen over us in the workspace. We all agreed, and then we walked out and drank drafts of beer at a nearby sports pub.

Later, as I was returning from the bathroom, I found that the music, though still unobtrusive, had grown louder in the bar, and that the place had taken on a rudderless air, one that seemed to fit the mood of our sudden detachment. I felt a surge of grief as I stood on the threshold. There was something final in that red, ill-lit scene, and I could already imagine our future as strangers in the metropolis.

Walking home to my prostitutes in upper Mowbray, and thinking of Le Roi's wife and what she owned, I thought maybe it was all for the best. I flagged down a cab and fell asleep on the passenger seat, waking later with the cab driver pulling on my sleeve, his headlights piercing the wrought-iron gate of my complex.

Two weeks after my retrenchment, I spent a portion of my severance package renting out a Czech boy and girl I found on the internet. This was on a night I couldn't sleep, and just a few days after reading *Equinox*, a novel by Samuel R. Delany that I'd loaned out from the library, in which a sea captain enslaves a pair of blond, teenage twins. I'd sent the email in a moment of inattention, without really expecting a reply, but only minutes later my cellphone went off on my desk. The voice on the line sounded younger than me. We set up a time, and I transferred the money using an EFT.

When they arrived, I prodded Ivan and Lenka as they screwed on my sleeper couch. Later, I came on my fingers as I watched her reaching her climax. We ate leftover roast chicken with seeded rolls after that, and Lenka made us look up her blog, which was a collection of naked children wearing animal masks in a Scandinavian forest, all of them captured in high-resolution images and supported by macabre music: a trip-hop playlist, she later explained. I took an old Ativan in the bathroom, about half a milligram's worth, and burned hash oil in an incense burner. It took us five minutes to get high from the smoke, and then we each took turns in the shower before Lenka and I lay on our sides on the couch. I jabbed my tongue under the soft hood of her clit and she clamped her thighs around my neck, and then, for close to five minutes, we tongued circles around each other's assholes. She took me in her mouth after that, pushed down as far as she could take me, then drew back to pull the tip of my stick out of her lips with a pop. Dipping back down, she masturbated me, her wrist rising in speed, and when she leaned back to pop me out of her mouth again, patting her palm firmly against my balls, I ejaculated across her forehead. Recuperating, I instructed Ivan to go down on her while I watched. He did, and when he tired of it, he pushed himself into her anus. I fell half-asleep with him grunting before waking up in a daze a few minutes later. Then I walked over to them and lowered myself into her mouth again. Her lips clutched me like a fist, and my right thigh trembled before I shot into Ivan's hair. Later, when I entered Lenka, I felt her fingers pressing down on my skin, drawing circles on my sweat, each digit pushing me forward. She lay below me, feeling like a delicate wound around the head of my penis, and as I felt her flesh widening, I pounded deeper into her, imagining I could burrow us through to something vast and embracing.

The next morning, I awoke on the sleeper couch. Lenka and Ivan had left sometime during the night. The living-room window had been left open to release the hash smoke, and for a moment I couldn't recall what month it was. I could hear the main road coming to life again, the taxis heading up to town with commuters and students, and, except for the dent the three of us had left on my single mattress, everything around me felt the same way it had the previous day.

FOURTH PART

WE NEVER HEAR FROM THE UGLY MAN AGAIN. I guess there isn't much else to say about him. He's just one of this city's many ciphers, we decide, one of the strange things that happen in the alleyways of the Southern Peninsula. Ruan speculates that he's a deposed president, and Cissie says he's the advisor to one. In any case, the money is retracted from our account, laundered most likely, and he never comes back for the ARVs. We decide to call him Ambroise Paré, after the man he admires, and Cissie says we should make masks out of his face. To the three of us, our planned meeting with Ethelia takes on an inevitable air, although we don't discuss it much. Cissie goes back to work; Ruan and I hang out.

Ethelia shows up at Cissie's place around a week later, on a Sunday afternoon. She knocks three times and finds the three of us sitting on the floor, each somehow sober. Cissie closes the door behind her. When she sees me, I wave at her and Ethelia smiles back.

I've never seen her close up before. She's dressed in a matching denim top and jeans. Cissie walks to the bedroom to get the package we retrieved for her from the safety deposit box. We had gone straight there—a private security company on Orange

Street—after having left the house in Woodstock. We hadn't really been surprised to discover that Ambroise had prepared the way for us. We only had to present them with the letter.

Ruan's reading an old comic book, an effort to calm his nerves. He's had this issue since he was twelve, he says, and he's let me have a look at it a few times. Half its pages are falling out, and it's about the Silver Surfer. The superhero wakes up on an alien planet, stranded without his surfboard, the source of his energy. Close to the end, he tries to sell his memories for a way out, but gets cheated by an agency that converts them to video.

I watch him from the couch. Ruan closes the comic book and places it carefully on the table. Cissie returns with the package and hands it to Ethelia, who receives it with both hands.

What is it?

Cissie turns to us. We don't know, she says, but it's yours.

Is it from my father?

Cissie doesn't reply. Ruan and I don't say anything, either. I realize I've never imagined Ethelia as having a voice.

My aunt told me my father was an important man, she says. Then she shakes the parcel. Can I open it?

It's yours, Cissie says.

Ethelia opens the package and money spills out, scattering on Cissie's floor. It's several wads of two-hundred-rand notes, followed by an ID and a passport.

Ethelia bends over to pick up the money, and for a moment it's as if she's back with her concrete pieces again—arranging them into another secret empire. Ruan, Cissie and I lean down to help, and Ethelia laughs as she handles the money. She laughs at the images of herself in the passport and ID.

So who knew? Cissie says. You're a Canadian.

I search the kitchen drawers and find rubber bands for the notes. Then I try to count the money, but it's too much to guess at a glance. We pack it up in bundles.

Ethelia stands with the package flat against her chest. My

aunt will be happy, she says, before going quiet. Then she looks up again. You've seen my father, haven't you?

Yes.

I guess all three of us say this at once.

Then Ruan and Cissie look at me and I go on.

We saw him, I say, and he wanted us to give you this.

Ethelia nods. Did he say anything about coming to my aunt's? I shake my head.

Then Ethelia looks down and nods. She starts to turn.

Wait, Cissie says, hold on. I have an idea.

She leaves the room and returns with a piece of paper and a sharpened pencil. Taking Ethelia by the hand, she leads her to the coffee table, kicking away an empty water bottle we were using for huffing. Ruan and I lean closer.

We watch them. Cissie asks Ethelia to draw a picture of the planet. It's the lesson she's used in her daycare class, the one her students couldn't get right. Ethelia takes the pencil and touches it against the foolscap.

Cissie says, imagine you're away from your aunt, and imagine you're away from West Ridge Heights. She places a hand on Ethelia's shoulder. Imagine you're away from your envelope, and away from the three of us, also.

Then, when Ethelia starts to sketch an oval shape inside the page's margins, Cissie says: imagine you're drawing a map into all of us.

In the morning, around seven, I email my landlord and tell him I want out of my twelve-month lease. I've come to accept that this has to be done. François replies that it's fine, it won't cause much hassle, he'll start showing the place to people right away. I type back, great, and leave West Ridge with Ruan and Cissie still asleep.

Down at the parking-lot gate, I wait for a car taking someone to work or school, and trail after its brake lights. Then I take a taxi along Main Road to Obs.

There was another hospital strike, our driver says when we reach the first stop in Mowbray. The passengers are packed on the seats behind him: twenty-two of us crammed in a fog of mixed perfume. The driver describes the passing of his mother-in-law, whose lungs collapsed in a Golden Arrow bus the previous morning.

That's life, the driver says, before rolling down his window.

From my seat I look out at the racing tar, at the undulating roofs of the brazen storefronts, and I remember how, in my fourth year of high school, my biology teacher took a flying class on the coast of Natal, and discovered a lesson for us in the air above Richards Bay. Her name was Mrs. Mathers, and when she returned to our class the following week, she told us how the Earth was gutted open with so many new graves for paupers, that when the clouds parted, they revealed a view from the sky that looked like a giant honeycomb. Then she watched everyone's expression. Mrs. Mathers was a part-time student of our emotional development. My classmates and I were known as the Math One class, relied upon for acuity but not much else, and we were only eighteen in number. Our teacher told us each grave was meant to contain the bodies of twenty adults.

She said to us, that is HIV.

I get off at Anzio and walk down past Lower Main. I use a round black tag to get inside my building, walk up two flights of stairs and let myself into my flat. The place feels like a storage room. It's dead still and airless. I open a window and drop myself on the bed.

Then I try to doze off and fail.

I peel my phone from my pocket and hold it in my palm. It's open on the text messenger. I remember Bhut' Vuyo's first message to me.

Lindanathi, you've come of age, it said.

It's been almost ten years. That's how long Luthando's been turning into powder inside the Earth. I rub my hand over my face and spend another minute looking at my cellphone. Then I close my eyes and try for sleep again, but nothing comes.

Later, when I try to use the toilet, I get the same feeling. Nothing makes its way out of me as I squat over the porcelain, and I feel time slowing down again. I lift the cistern lid and pull on the lever to flush. Then I walk back to the kitchen and drink a glass of water with ice. In the end, I manage to get two hours of sleep.

Waking up again, I text Cecelia, asking her if she wants anything. I've accepted I'll have to give most of my belongings away.

I wait, but there's no reply, so I turn my computer on. Then I get up from my desk and walk over to the lav again to take a leak. You've never been happy here, I say, observing myself in the speckled mirror. Then I light a cigarette and try to do the dishes, but my hands start trembling. I drain the water and make a cup of tea instead.

Sitting back at my desk, I click on a button that sends the browser to my blog. There's a draft of a post I wrote more than a week ago. I read through it again from the top. This is how it goes:

> Last night I projected myself out of my body, going through more loops than is usual for me. I've forgotten the first loop, which is common. The second one took place at a party some-where. No one seemed impressed by my ability to fly for short amounts of time, or to jump really high above the ground. Flying feels like trying to stay awake when you're extremely tired and half-asleep. I discovered fear is what inhibits flight. I was an artist in the second loop and met another artist. He held my face

and looked into my eyes and said, yes, it's true, you're dreaming. He was impressed. He talked about it at length. This made me too aware of being in a loop, however, and the loop disintegrated and I found myself at my father's house. There was a man pacing in the backyard; when I followed him, he dug a hole in the ground and disappeared. I became aware of dreaming again, and feeling exhausted. I tested myself by jumping over a heap of sharp rocks. Then I tried to pull a spider towards me with my mind. It moved, but it could've been the wind. Eventually, I heard a voice telling me it was fine, that I could still do it. I felt relief, but at the same time fear because I wouldn't be able to do it again. I was struck by the idea of being in what you know is a dream, but without capabilities, with a fragmented memory and an unstable reality. I thought maybe this is what schizophrenia is. I didn't remember having taken off my shirt, but I was topless. I'd had enough, but I couldn't will myself to wake up and this made me panic. Then I found the shirt in front of the house, and as I picked it up and turned around, that's when I woke up to now, in bed, my heart beating fast. I recognized this as reality because of the new weight I felt coursing through me, my body recognizing the Earth's gravitational field. Then I opened my eyes to find everything in place.

My blog has no audience and I've never shared a link for the purpose of gaining one. I scroll back up and click on the publish button.

Then my intercom goes off. I can't stand the sound it makes, so I rush over to it whenever it clangs. I stub my toe on the way to the door.

It's a guy from the courier: I have your delivery, he says.

I put on a pair of slops and walk out of the door, and, as I'm turning the key, I get a text from Cissie saying they just got up half-an-hour ago: they're waiting for a taxi along Main Road. Ruan's walking her to work. I text back saying, all right, and that I've just received the pill package. Cissie says to meet them in Mowbray with the box.

I won't go in today, she says. I'll just tell Lauren I'm taking my leave.

I meet the delivery man downstairs. He's this older guy, a Shona man, he tells me, and I nod. He's Zimbabwean the way Ruan's grandparents used to be Rhodesian, I think. He gives me a pen and I scrawl my name across his clipboard.

Then I take the box back upstairs, drop it on my bed and take off my clothes. I try to do push-ups on the concrete floor, but stop when I reach eleven, feeling my heart race and my muscles wither from my skeleton.

In the shower, the water comes out warm, and more than once I hear the copper pipes groaning like they're being pulled apart from opposite ends. Then I close my eyes and listen to the water smacking the tiles between my feet. I try to disappear into the patter until the water runs cold on my skin. This will be my last shower here.

Twenty minutes later, I meet Cissie and Ruan outside Cissie's place of work, her daycare center in Mowbray. Cissie says she's collected two weeks of holiday; that they have a new girl to make up the gap. I tell them I have the pills inside my bag. We buy bottled water at the nearby KFC and break a stem of khat at a rounded corner table. Then the three of us take one of the taxis heading from Wynberg to town.

In half an hour, we reach the taxi rank. Our driver backs into the bay marked for Wynberg and we get out and walk past a row of Cell C containers into Cape Town Station. I tell Ruan and Cecelia about my uncle Bhut' Vuyo, and how he's hatched a harebrained plan to see me today. I say this slowly, to make the two of them laugh, and then I shrug. I tell them I won't be long. I don't mention I've made no plans to return to the city.

We find the new public rest rooms, smelling like a heap of feces coated in disinfectant, and Cissie waits outside while Ruan and I take the last stall in the men's.

We've always broken the seals on these boxes together. Today will mark the last occasion. Ruan and I split the package of ARVs between us and then flush the toilet. The boom of the train announcer wraps around my head as we walk out, and for a moment, everyone on the buffed floor seems to stop and glance up at us. I pause, but then decide it doesn't matter either way.

We say goodbye on Adderley Street. Ruan and Cissie want to get Ruan's things from his uncle's firm, so they cross over to the Absa ATM while I walk up towards the Grand Parade. The sun feels noncommittal in its bond to our planet today, spilling out light as gray as bath water. On Strand, I cut through the bus depot, skipping in front of a Golden Arrow bus grunting towards Atlantis. Further down, I walk past a vegetable stall, a hairdresser's tent, and a medicine stand displaying a large plant bulb and bottles of herbal tonic. I climb up the steel staircase that leads back to the taxi rank. It's the longer route, which allows me to take down a smoke on the way. I buy my third cigarette on the platform, a Stuyvesant red, from a wrinkled woman wearing a blue *doek*. She sells Cadbury éclairs and flavored water. Next to her, a muscular man in shades and a pea coat leans up against a sooty column, holding a hot Sony Ericsson phone. It's still on and he's hawking it for a grand, he says. I pay the woman and walk past them, looking for a taxi headed up the West Coast. Eventually, I find one headed for Parklands, which goes past Table View. It's a red Caravelle, and I settle myself in the back seat, my head leaning up against the window. I take out my cellphone and wait for the taxi to fill up. Usually they take a while.

Eventually, a girl with red-tinted hair, wearing a green gym tunic, takes the seat in front of me, filling up the passenger count. I hear the music thumping into her skull from her headphones, a kwaito artist, famous for being a minor and beating a drug case. *We no longer sleep*, he sings, as the taxi grumbles to life around us. *We no longer sleep*, he repeats, when we start out of the taxi rank. We pass the vendors with their Niknaks and Nollywood rugs, squeezing ourselves between more taxis streaming in from Victoria Road. Then I hear him for the last time. *We no longer sleep*, he sings, as we turn into Christiaan Barnard and the roof of the Good Hope Center reveals itself, rising like a dull and blind observatory on our right.

In the end, I guess I was never cut out to be a journalist. During my second year at university, I took an assignment to interview a pop star for my final-term project. The man was part of what was being called a revival in indigenous Venda music, and I wanted to ask him about its representation in the papers. I found the coverage of the band exploitative, but my saying so didn't go down well with the singer. We fumbled our way through my introduction of this angle, before he caught on that I wasn't altogether worth his time. He looked at his wristwatch a few times and asked me for my age. It was clear that I had no inclination towards his music, he said, and perhaps no inclination towards music at all. No soul, he later improvised, when we were both loosened up by our first tray of gin. He fell silent and I followed his gaze out to the main road. It was a bright, sunlit Tuesday afternoon, and cars were driving past with their

windows down, hurling snatches of summer anthems into the
heat. We were sitting in a café in Rondebosch, full of North
Americans, caffeine and the smell of chocolate brownies. He
was struggling to log onto the network. Our second drinks had
arrived and the alcohol was touching my head.

I felt my interest piqued at the mention of metaphysics. I
asked him if the soul was important to Venda culture, and if he
knew anyone else like me who didn't have one. He looked across
the table at me with the combination of irritation and disgust I'd
come to expect from older men in the field. I thought he would
get up and walk out, but when I offered him another drink, he
accepted. We had the third round in silence and later, outside
the café, we shook hands and I gave him directions to the V&A
Waterfront, where he wanted to buy clothes from a Gap and
Fabiani sale. We parted after that, and I walked back to campus.
Then I realized I hadn't managed to switch my recorder on for
the interview.

In bed, later that week, I couldn't recall any of his songs
by name, and a day after that I decided to deregister from my
degree. It wasn't how I was meant to meet the world. On campus, the curriculum advisor, a loud, jovial American man who
wore glasses and had a tight white ponytail, asked me to state my
reasons. I told him I liked reading, but had no interest in writing.
I wanted a career without people skills, I joked, but he didn't
laugh. He looked at a copy of my matric results, achieved at a
stern boarding school in Natal where there had been nothing
else to do but study, and he shouted: science.

Our driver shifts his stick down and changes lanes towards Civic.
We pass Old Marine Drive before we swerve into an Engen to
fill up with gas. Two petrol attendants walk up to the driver and
offer to shake his hand. Ta T-Man, both of them say, *hoezit, groot-
man?* The driver nods, handing each a twenty-rand note with the

shake. I sit and watch them as they talk. Then I get a text from Cissie telling me Ruan managed to avoid his uncle at the firm. The driver rolls up his window, after that, and we pull off again, on our way to Du Noon.

What will I remember about my friends? The good times, I suppose, even though they didn't always appear good at the time. I'll remember West Ridge Heights. I'll remember Ruan telling us that he'd made an evaluation of our personalities, and that he'd plotted them on a hundred-year time scale and concluded that, in the near future, it would become easier for the three of us to detect the defects carried by other people, their fears and deceits, and because of this, we would have a map to locate others like ourselves, who'd been marked in similar ways.

I remember agreeing with him, that day, and maybe each of us had felt more hopeful than usual. Ruan, Cissie and I had been huffing paint thinner at Ruan's place in Sea Point. Elaborating, Ruan said that after leaving school, he'd lost his natural ability to cultivate relationships with other human beings, but because of the two of us, he felt this being restored to him.

I guess that was something I could understand.

It was something the three of us shared.

In Wynberg, when we came around to meeting each other for the first time, it was with a measure of caution, and the results surprised us. We'd each resigned ourselves to passing by, whenever we met other people, by then. Things had happened to each of us along the way, I suppose, and, as we stood and mumbled by the serving table that afternoon, watching as the rest of the members bonded over biscuits in Mary's basement, there was no question of our getting romantically involved with each other. In that short time, we'd seemed to have agreed, with a quiet and complicit relief, that we were somehow too wrecked, and that we had met within obviously wrecked circumstances. Ruan, Cissie and I had never owned up to the things we'd had to do in order to keep seeing each other, in those first few weeks of friendship; never admitted to what it was, where it was, and who it was that we were detaching ourselves from. This secrecy hadn't been incidental, I later felt, but was meant to maintain something unknowable in each of us: a corner we could keep divested of goodwill, without any breach in conscience, at the times we had to hurt each other to spare ourselves.

Though that hardly ever happened.

Which is what I'll remember, too.

I'll remember how, two years ago, Ruan began to vomit and wouldn't stop even after an hour of heaving on his bathroom floor. He'd had another threat from his uncle and another letter from the bank, and he'd been drinking Gin Rickeys at a bar down the road from his flat. Cissie and I tried to catch up with him when we arrived; we each ordered two drinks at a time, but soon we ran out of money.

Outside the bar, Ruan began to laugh as he lit up a filter. He waved his hand across the panorama of the beach, and then inwards across the promenade and the traffic. It was in the early evening and the sky was tinted a burning pink, with a streak of orange cirrus hanging over the horizon. The streetlights were beginning to flicker on intermittently, as if roused from a deep sleep by our footsteps. Ruan hadn't talked about his uncle that day, and Cissie and I knew he wouldn't. The three of us were quiet as the cars raced past, a play of light obscuring the faces of the drivers. I imagined them to be headed to Camps Bay for sundowners, or to dinner reservations in the center of town.

We stumbled together. Cissie and I kept Ruan propped up between us. We passed our first cigarette quickly and lit up another one. Then Ruan pointed us towards his flat: he said he wanted to crash.

There were windows on two of the walls in Ruan's living room and they both looked out over the vista of the Atlantic. Most of them were opened wide, pushed out to the hilt of the hinges, and Ruan had given us specific instructions to leave them that way. He said that sometimes the windows, left ajar, could make the flat seem like a moving structure, as if, sitting alone in his living room at the helm of his glass-topped coffee table, he was in control of something large and industrial, and that, by his efforts alone, he could lift it up and maneuver it out to sea.

When I sat down on his bean-bag that night, the walls seemed to stand up in my stead, the windows sliding hazily down off the bricks. The sounds of the traffic, the promenade and the ocean all reached into the living room and mingled with the noises of Ruan and Cissie looking for thinners in the cabinets. Then the windows slowly readjusted themselves on the walls. When I blinked again, closing my eyes for longer intervals, my head had the feeling of being steered in small, concentric circles. I laid it back on the bean-bag and watched Ruan and Cissie from an inverted perspective, their frames slightly elongated, their feet standing where their chins should've hung. Ruan's hands shot down to his mouth and he pushed himself back from the counter, and for a moment Cissie and I stared at each other through his absence. Then we followed him to the bathroom, and there we found his fig trees inside the bath tub. He had a collection of small potted plants he'd splattered with his own blood, the aim being to spread himself to the world through the different birds that ate them.

I won't forget that.

The first time LT and I saw people having sex was through my neighbors' bedroom window. This was back home, at my mother's house in eMthatha, and we'd giggled so loudly that the guy, blond and stocky—with his face flushed red—had banged on the window and screamed, telling us to fuck off. We'd both had our turn with girls after that and I guess I had a few more than LT did before he turned to a boy in his neighborhood. He would remember it better than I would, although I doubt by a very wide margin.

I remember our uncles, with their gold teeth and beer breath, and how they'd find the two of us at every family gathering, hoist us on their knees, and goad us about becoming men. I'd smile at them while my stomach sank. I'd learned early to be deceitful with older drunks. They got on the bottle and treated you like anyone else—not a Model C who didn't know his clan name from his asshole.

I was scared to go home for circumcision. Most of us were. We'd grown up hearing stories about what could go wrong. There was the initiate who'd had the head fall off his shaft while he swam upstream in the Mthatha River, and the one who had to be rushed to hospital because his wound wasn't properly dressed. Each winter, the *Dispatch* reported on guys like us dropping in droves. It wasn't the pain: we knew that would pass. I'd just never pictured myself as one of the guys who'd come out the other side—someone who could get along up there.

I also knew that, really, I was scared of being close to LT. The rumors about him had spread and he'd been set apart. I didn't want people to mix us up, to look at me the same way they did him. When the Mda house came under pressure to make a man out of its sissy son, I kept away—I crossed my arms in Cape Town.

LT was younger than me, and he didn't believe in what they said—what you had to become to be a man—but he still called to ask me for my help. I told him to go in June, and that I would follow as soon as I handed in my assignments. Well, I never went back. I switched off my phone a week later and abandoned him up there. Later, they said LT fought them and that's what killed him.

Often, I've thought about how I wouldn't know if that was true; about how I was absent during his last hours, and about how, when he died, my arms were still crossed in Cape Town.

One year after I graduated from Tech, and a week before the sixth anniversary of LT's death, I infected myself with HIV in the laboratories. That's how I became a reactive. I never had the reactions I needed for myself, and I couldn't react when LT called to me for help, so I gave my own body something it couldn't flee from. Now here's your older brother and murderer, Luthando. His name is Lindanathi and his parents got it from a girl.

FIFTH PART

IT TAKES THE TAXI LESS THAN AN HOUR TO REACH
Du Noon. Even with three children, Bhut' Vuyo and his wife
spend most of their lives making a home inside a shipping container. This isn't an unusual way to live in Du Noon. The containers here have multiplied since my last stay, in '95, and I can
see them from the taxi as we drive in: hair salons, eateries and
phone shops, all of them packaged inside steel boxes like time
capsules. Ta T-Man sticks in a CD full of house MP3s, and, as
we push deeper into the township, I can't help but peer into
the dim insides of the crates. It feels the same as seeing regular
poverty, but cut into sections and prepared for export. In front
of the containers, lined up like mechanical sentries, portable toilets stoop under the slanting sunlight, four for every dozen containers. It's supposedly a temporary measure, meant to tide the
people over until after the upcoming local election.

The container I'm traveling to is red, corrugated and a source
of concern for its owner. Even at a glance, you can tell it's old
and falling apart. Bhut' Vuyo spends a few days each month
extending it with sheets of discarded zinc, sometimes driving
his lorry to Blouberg, where he scours the shore for bits of
wood, planks, or anything he can find that isn't too rotted from
the ocean. He's learned to make his way with what he finds, discarded by the hands of others. My uncle is a large and laughing

man, but if you get close enough to him, it isn't hard to tell that he's walked into places that surprised him with bloodshed.

I arrive at the corner of Ingwe and Bhengu Streets just after three o'clock. It's a weekday and quieter than usual. I spot a makeshift pit latrine, its walls made from corrugated iron and wood, leaning precariously at the side of Bhut' Vuyo's home. The clouds have allowed the sun free rein, and its light slams brilliantly into the ribbed metal, the earth still muddy at the base, with spikes of chopped plank exposed. Flies hover in a cloud around the structure. I find my uncle sitting on a crate in front of his container, observing his work with a quart between his ankles. His beer belly flows over his thighs, the sweat on his head sparkling as it catches the light. You can tell by the way he looks at the tin that it's a fresh triumph. He's sweaty and lively when he sees me. When he extends his hand, it isn't to shake my own, but to draw me into an embrace. Welcome home, he says with warmth, and I smile, not knowing what else to do.

The first day at my uncle's place comes and goes without consequence. He doesn't mention his message to me. I help him with the pit latrine, which caves in shortly after my arrival, and for supper he fries us beef livers and onions, dished generously with pap and bread crusts. I wash the dishes in a yellow bucket, and afterwards I unroll *umkhukhu* on the vinyl tiles. We share a Courtleigh and he tells me how his wife has taken the children to visit her parents in Langa. Outside, the township comes to life with the sun having set. I watch the smoke hovering around the mountain of my uncle on his bed. There are indications that parts of him still belong out there. His forearms bear scars from stripping cars with their engines still hot, back when he worked as mechanic in a chop shop in Khwezi Park. His movements are quick, an instinct he's retained from his days in the syndicate.

We'll talk after her return, he says, and I nod.

I open the door to flick out the cigarette stub and stare with surprise at how close the moon looks. Inside, Bhut' Vuyo blows out the candle and I coil myself inside a blanket and a towel. Soon, the container fills up with the sound of his labored breathing; I trip into unsettled dreams after he goes down.

The next two days pass just as quietly. Bhut' Vuyo leaves for Blouberg while I sleep on his floor. I don't see him until the early evening, when we cook and sit for our supper and a beer. He prepares dumplings and then samp. He promises to keep us chin-deep in meat this entire week, and, during meals, he keeps me abreast on who comes and goes in the community. I recognize Ta T-Man, the taxi driver, from one of his faster stories. He shows me a scar on his forearm. Ta T-Man and his men were trying to introduce a *nyaope* cartel in the neighborhood, he says, but the Cape took little interest in the drug. I get close to telling him about my ARVs, but I decide against it. I have an idea he still thinks I'm a student.

During the day, when Bhut' Vuyo disappears, I take Industrial and lie on the floor to read. He buys the *Daily Voice*, which he uses to wallpaper the container, and on the walls I read about gangs spraying bullets across the streets of Lavender Hill, or I read about Delft, where the women have started to mark *tik* houses with large X's on the garages. The rest of Cape Town starts to feel distant beyond these pages, surrounded by uncertainty and receding into memory. There are other times when I don't read. I lie on the floor with my eyes closed, listening to the sounds of the neighborhood. When I run out of airtime, I decide to go without it. Then I spend more time listening to what Du Noon might have to say to me.

On Saturday, Bhut' Vuyo and I finish up with the latrine. He fetches a box of tools from Milnerton and this makes our job go faster. We work hastily, barely a word passing between us, and get done in just under three hours. Every time I lay a plank down, I feel myself filling up with relief and gratitude, thankful that I missed the spade work before I arrived. Digging the hole must've taken a fortnight, at the very least, and I'm careful not to bring this up with him, in case he finds more work for me to take up.

His latrine is more of a gesture than a necessity. It's a political project, I realize, and in reality a lot less functional than the toilets that insult him. The residents on his block have developed an efficient ecosystem with the Portaloos, and, when Bhut' Vuyo leaves for Blouberg, I try one out for myself. The formaldehyde has turned a brownish green, meaning it's stopped neutralizing the odor, and it smells like the combined waste of eight households. I hold my breath as much as I can before I give up. It's a public toilet, after all, I tell myself. I rub one of Bhut' Vuyo's papers soft between my knuckles and wipe myself. I've been told by the neighbors that my uncle's family makes use of the toilets, too, and that he's a fool for putting up that zinc wreck in his yard. I listen to this with a mixture of pride and embarrassment. Here, no one else seems to bother with gestures any more. Perhaps this counts for something, I think.

Later, we share a quart outside the container. They should be burned, Bhut' Vuyo says.

Standing and facing Bhengu Street, the two of us wait for our turn with the water. I follow his gaze, tracing it to the blue and gray plastic toilets that line the narrow street. They're built wide and tall, and from where I'm standing I can see the marks defacing one of them. Like Bhut' Vuyo wants, someone has held a fire to it. This must've been a weak flame, however.

We aren't wealthy people, Nathi, he says, you know that.

I nod that I do.

We cross the road to the communal tap, which stands on a concrete square in a barren field. Goalposts made from carved branches have been erected at each end, but no one has any interest in playing games in Du Noon any more. Bhut' Vuyo lets the water run into a bucket and we go back to the house and pour Omo washing powder over our palms. When we sit back down and face the street again, another woman has taken her place at the tap. She fills a yellow enamel basin without handles. Two small children hang on her legs and she keeps kicking them away. They laugh at her scolding and run towards the goalposts. The water feels cool in the heat. Bhut' Vuyo says the Sunlight soap is only used for washing our bodies. We scoop up more washing powder for our palms.

They should be burned, he repeats, before shifting on his crate. We aren't wealthy, Nathi, but we aren't prisoners, he says.

I dry my hands against my pants. It smells like a clothesline under my fingernails.

I know things can be worse, Bhut' Vuyo says. In Khayelitsha? The toilets don't have walls. This is a place a man's wife must relieve herself. There, with men and children watching. He shakes his head and spits into the ground.

In town, Cissie once told us about an artist named Adrian Blackwell. He'd created a portable toilet with a one-way mirror and installed it on a pavement in Toronto and Ottawa. While the door of the cube was reflective on the outside, the person on the bowl could see out into the traffic. I guess Cissie would've called this the collective unconscious. Adrian Blackwell never gave any indication of having heard of Khayelitsha, but in his way, he'd recreated it. I doubt Bhut' Vuyo would find any of this of interest, however, so I decide to terminate the thought.

I take a look around us instead.

Despite the temperament of our conversation, Du Noon is filled with warmth and sunshine today. It's a Saturday, which means the routine is mild and the commute is halved. Taxis play loud house music as they wheel about, picking up passengers dressed in their best Saturday clothes. The women's figures are fit snugly into white slim jeans and some of them have sprayed their weaves, making them gleam in the morning light. Their lips are painted red and sometimes hot pink, and a strong air of confidence radiates from them. They stroll towards a taxi if it doesn't stop at their feet. One woman walks by wearing a pair of hoop earrings. Each circle glimmers in the sunlight.

I turn to Bhut' Vuyo. I say, at least people are still alive, here.

I must sound bored or unconvinced, because Bhut' Vuyo just laughs in response. The laugh itself sounds sparse and cold. I can't trace humor in the eyes or enjoyment around the mouth. Thankfully, it passes quickly. He claps his hands together.

That's not living, he says.

Then he looks at my face and smiles. My uncle pats the side of my leg. Tell me about your studies, he says. Tell me about life at the university. One day you're going to change all of this, aren't you? He lets out another laugh and his smile stays on his face for a long time. You and your whites, he says.

Sis' Nosizi, Bhut' Vuyo's wife, is due to return to us in Du Noon on the Sunday, just a day after we finish up with the latrine, bringing the two younger children with her. In preparation for her arrival, we do what we can for the container. I put up more *Daily Voice* spreads on the walls, more shootings and *tik* dens, and replace the ones I wiped with and soaked in the pools of formaldehyde. For his part, Bhut' Vuyo arrives back early from his work in Blouberg with two packs of beef shanks. He rips the plastic between his teeth and whistles as he rinses the meat in the water bucket. I cut a square of Holsum and watch it melt in the frying pan. The Primus stove is broken, parked outside by the crates, so we use a gas two-plate for our cooking. Bhut' Vuyo busies himself with his specialty.

There is a reason I called you here, Nathi, he says to me.

I listen.

My wife, he says. You mustn't be scared.

I nod. I've always known Sis' Nosizi is a diviner. What she

does for a living doesn't intimidate me. I look forward to hearing her stories.

Then Bhut' Vuyo changes his tone and licks his fingers. He whistles over the pan and reaches for the salt shaker. Pass me the stock, he tells me. You know nothing, my boy.

I pass it. We laugh and prepare just enough for us to eat.

When Sis' Nosizi returns, she looks at me for a long time. Then she embraces me and tears find their way down both our necks.

My circumcision is discussed only once. We set a date for late December. It's decided that I'll go in with their eldest son, Luvuyo. He arrives in Du Noon a week early. I let him greet his parents and siblings for about an hour, and then we walk down to Magasela's to buy a crate of quarts. We drink until we turn half-blind, and then we roar our way home. We'll have a small ceremony, they've told us, and the next morning our hair is shaved off by our neighbor. Ta Kader lives in a blue container opposite Bhut' Vuyo's. He crosses the road with a bowl of water and a pack of Lion razor blades. Taking sips from a warm Black Label dumpy, he tells us jokes under the blinding sun.

We head out to Cape Town Station after that. Outside the bus terminal, Luvuyo and I prepare to board a coach heading to eMthatha. Bhut' Vuyo has business in town, he tells us, looking out of place in front of the station's modern blue signage. We had a moment to talk just before we left Du Noon. He asked me to pass his gratitude on to my family back home, and I said to him that I would. His family had worn too thin to carry Luvuyo through initiation, he explained, and I nodded to indicate my understanding of their circumstances.

Now I get ready to leave Cape Town. I think of my friends as Luvuyo and I board the beeping Intercape bus outside. I think about where Ruan and Cecelia could be on a day like today—a day in which I finally take my leave of this city. We never made it out to the Eastern Cape to grow khat in our idyll like we wanted to; but we still have many years left before the end of our paths. I board the bus before I get ensnared in the thought, finding an empty seat near the back. Then I shrug and wish the two of them the best.

There's a young couple dozing under a blanket to my right. They have their hands buried between each other's thighs and are breathing heavily. Luvuyo nudges me as he walks past and points at them with a grin. *Naaiers*, he says, sitting down in the seat behind me.

I grin. I guess I wish myself the best, too. I wish Luvuyo the same. Leaning back, I close my eyes before we start moving. The trip is fifteen hours long, they say, and our journey will push us across a thousand kilometers of our country. Luvuyo and I have been told everything we need to know. We'll return from this journey as new men, they said.

We do. Three weeks later my family has a small celebration for us back home, in eMthatha, and after *umgidi wethu*, we make it back to Du Noon in early January. For a while, Luvuyo and I hang around the neighborhood, wearing our uniform and doing the rounds to meet with other guys who've just come out. It isn't the way it used to be, everyone complains. You get men as young as fourteen, now, and they bring guns into the circles we open to greet one another, pressing *amakrwala* for buttons and brandy. We give it two weeks before we decide it isn't worth the hassle, or maybe even the risk. I change out of my blazer and newsboy cap and wonder how much I could hawk them for.

Towards the end of the month Luvuyo takes a taxi out of Du Noon, but I decide to stick around for a while. I take Industrial when everyone's out, and then I start walking the neighborhood on my own, asking around for anyone who might have work.

In the end, I take a job at a *spaza*. It's in a double container just around the corner from Bhut' Vuyo's, a place popular for pushing out cigarettes and five-rand airtime. It isn't anything serious. It keeps my shoulders above water when we reach the end of the month. I split myself between the cleaning and the selling, and sometimes I'll go behind the counter and take a look at my boss's books; I'll do a few numbers for her.

There's a lot of kids who pass by the shop. Most of them get sent from home to buy bread, airtime, or bleach—household items for their overworked mothers. These *laaities* like to act smooth if you let them. They'll bring a half-loaf down to a quarter and then burn the change on *entjies* and rolling paper. Sometimes I serve them and other times I don't. It depends on the kind of day I'm having when I get on my shift. I serve their older brothers, too—guys who come from my block and the ones next to ours. They lope up to my container with a million-rand scheme burning out of their eyes, each with a plan to turn Du Noon on its head. They ask me for deodorant and cigarettes, mostly, and I slide them packets of free condoms too. My boss used to be a school teacher; she makes us do that if we have them around.

Sometimes, one of the guys will pocket the jackets and hang around the store for a while, waiting for me to get off my shift. We'll *dap* an *entjie* outside the container and he'll tell me to come around to the corner for quarts, and that it's been a while since the *ous* saw me playing pool at Ta Ace's. If I'm off the next day, I'll tag along with him. I'll drop the keys on the counter and ignore my boss's glares, her warnings. We'll take the main road, most of the time, and go past the inn, where the taxis crank their bass so high they could move the walls of a thousand houses backwards; and it's at times like these, with the evening sky tinted the bright color of a new coal fire, that things seem possible, even for us down here.

Then one day, without any warning, I remember the man we

once met on that cold night in Mowbray; I remember Monsieur Paré and the mask he wore on the day the three of us, Ruan, Cecelia and I, took our seats with him. It happens on a wet, gray morning, and when I think of him, I think of his daughter, Ethelia, as well.

Friday shifts are the longest at the shop, so I always make sure to take down two cigarettes on the way, just to keep the tar from rising up to my face. Today, I smoke the first one on Bhengu, and when I cross over to Eagle Street, passing by a pack of school children who climb, one after the other, into the doors of a peeling Hi-Ace, I hear the first noises from the mob. I nod at the driver as I pass, one of Ta T-Man's new men, and when I take the corner into Nomzamo, my eyes smart and the wind stings when it flows into my throat. It's cold and scented with motor oil; heavy with the smell of burning rubber. Maybe there's been another strike, I think, but when I look around, no one seems torpid enough to be off the clock.

I keep walking.

I find the crowd a block away from my job; a small mob of around twenty people, and when I get closer, I hear them shouting over each other, hurling accusations about a pyramid scheme and talking about a man who'll later remind me of Paré. In the crowd, a few people hold up election posters. They've ripped them down from the containers which fortify the front end of Du Noon, at the beginning of Dumani Street, and the faces of the politicians have been blanked out with white paint. In the center of the mob, they have the offender sprawled on the ground. He looks no older than eighteen. Two tires smolder behind him in a small stack, the cause of the heady stink in the air. Three women, standing to my right and in front of an old man in stained overalls, say the boy was trying to torch the neighborhood, and that only a month ago he'd stolen money from Du Noon's pensioners, selling them a pyramid scheme called The Golden Fowl.

I nod, feeling I've got the gist of it.

Then I push myself deeper into the crowd and see him curled up on his side. He's a small man, wearing nothing but a light-green vest—something they say he lifted from the clothesline behind him. Turning over on his side, he starts to laugh, spitting into the ground and turning a clot of it into mud under his chin. He addresses the crowd at the same time, shouting about the coming of a man without a face. The crowd falls silent and we listen. He sinks his nails into the earth, digs up a fistful of soil, and hurls it over his head. He says we'll no longer be slaves, when the faceless man comes. Then he releases a stream of urine into the dust, and that's when they drive the first shopping trolley into his flank, scraping him across the earth. The women in front of me tell the men to go easy on him: to only teach the boy a lesson. *Ligeza eli*, they say, a madman, and then they tell the men to dress him in clothes after they're done. The men, themselves not much older than the offender, laugh, but agree to do so.

Then most of us turn back to our jobs. When I tell my boss what's happened in the street outside, she just grunts. Her eyes remain unmoved, her reading glasses fixed on the numbers in her book.

Look at where you are, she says, waving a hand at me. Then tell me what you find surprising about this.

I don't know how to respond, so I shrug. Then I crack my knuckles and take my place at her counter.

Not much, I say in the end, to her as well as myself.

I push an empty Kiwi shoe-polish tin under the stool to keep it from rocking. Through the doorway, I watch the rutted road die once more, before it comes back to life with our customers at lunchtime.

Time manages to pass after that, but I can't help thinking about it: all the things I heard and saw that day. Later, after they'd beaten up the offender—his name was Siseko—they told him to go home, but he hung around our neighborhood instead, walking the streets and taking long laps from Siya to Curry Street, holding conversations with himself about the man and his coming.

I drew a mask for him, once. He'd come over to buy an *entjie* for the doorman at Ta Ace's, where he'd started cleaning tables and floors. We went behind the container, and when I showed him the face I'd drawn on a piece of paper, he said I had the key. It was a sketch of Ambroise Paré—as I remembered him, at least—and Siseko laughed and called me the white man from Sis' Thoko's *spaza*. He said I had the key that would save all of us, and I guess I must've laughed too, since I didn't want to think any more than I had to about it. To me, Monsieur Paré had only been a parent, and Ethelia his daughter: a father.

We smoked in silence after that, and I remember feeling a sense of peace rushing into me as I watched him walking away with the mask. I knew I wouldn't be the only one to do him a favor that day, to make sure he sometimes landed on his feet. The community had taken him in, like it had done with me, and there was no need to be fearful of everything we didn't know.

Sometimes I still hear from Sis' Thobeka. I finally gave her that CD4-count sheet, believe it or not. They say the virus is arrested in my blood.

I took a taxi to town and wrote an email to Le Roi about it. It was a Tuesday. I walked up Long Street and made my way to the basement level of the African Women's Craft Market, just a block down from the Palm Tree Mosque, where I paid a five rand to the Rasta who manned the café counter.

Le Roi wrote back to me fast, telling me how he'd moved to the south of France. I was in luck, he said, since he'd taken my condition as a focus, restricting his research to non-progressors and a handful of immunes. It was a small lab in a middling college, however, and the only way he stayed afloat was by no longer having his South African wife to worry over. I didn't ask him about that, and he said nothing about the job she'd got me. In the end, we exchanged emails for about half an hour, and concluded that I wasn't a modern miracle. I was still reactive, just slow to develop the syndrome. I have a large number of antibodies, for reasons the two of us couldn't fathom.

It was the last time I ever spoke to André, and I suppose he was right in his diagnosis.

Still, before I left, I gave another five-rand coin to the Rasta and sat down to send one last message to Le Roi. I left the body of this email empty—the two of us had said everything there was to say—and linked him to a news article about the government's new Operational Plan. Dated the first of September, the government was reported as having finally relented, ending a five-year struggle: under increased pressure from a civil disobedience suit, the South African cabinet had ruled to provide free ARVs to the country's citizens. Most of us were still in disbelief. Sis' Thobeka, whom I'd called from a pay phone close to work, had held back tears, and Bhut' Vuyo had slapped a copy of the *Voice* against his thigh. The article said that the government planned to provide treatment for a hundred thousand of us by March the following year. Who knew? I thought. It was enough to believe them for now.

I left the café and took a taxi west from the station deck. Passing the Atlantic Seaboard, I thought about how many times I'd taken this same route, my backpack filled with pills that were meant to preserve my life and the lives of those who could afford it. How many of us were affected inside this taxi? Inside the metropolis? I looked at the assortment of heads in front of me and wondered who I would've sold to. Then I thought of my old clients. I thought of Ronny and Leonardo. I thought of Millicent, and I thought of Ta Lloyd and his wife.

Soon, the taxi approached Du Noon.

I felt relieved to be close to home, and later, as I settled down to sleep, I thought about our country's infection rate. I wondered if we'd been selected in particular for this trial. Perhaps HIV was a purge, I imagined, a brutal transition on the other side of which might lie a newer, stronger human species, one resistant to a thousand more ailments and vital enough to survive all the trials that were still germinating in the future. It was just an idea, but I thought that when the time came, those who knew might be looked upon to lead.

The following week, there was an article written about us slow progressors in the *City Press*. Sis' Thobeka, who called, encouraged me to go in for tests, and one of these days, I told her, I might surprise myself and do just that.

Just pull me away from Esona first. I know I haven't mentioned a single thing about her, but this is how all of that goes. The two of us meet on a clear, hot Saturday towards the end of my first November in Du Noon, before Luvuyo and I head up to eMthatha. I've just borrowed my uncle's lorry and driven it out to a park jam in Khayelitsha: a new hip-hop festival that goes on for half a day on a stage outside Mandela Park, on the corner of Oscar Mpetha and Govan Mbeki Roads. That morning, I turn a corner and spot the white Pick n Pay shopping bags which clutch the barbed wire like the flags of a different country, twisting their bodies to the tune of rap music and neglect. Closer, I start to feel the bass coming off the PA system, the thump murmuring against my windows. I pull in, shift down a gear and park close to the gathering. Then I walk to a nearby *spaza* for a warm pack of Amstels. I open a can and stash the rest in the van.

I meet Esona when I close the door of the van behind me and take out a Stuyve to suck in with the beer. She's on her own, the way Esona will always be on her own, and she has a canvas backpack sagging on her bright brown shoulders. When our eyes meet across the hoods of two busted-up Fords, each of us refuses to step down, to be the one who moves away, and so we stay like that for a while, feeling as close as forehead to forehead. Two *laaities* pick at discarded chicken bones on the tar between us, and Esona and I stare at each other over their backs for a while.

Eventually, she walks up to me and asks for a *skyf*. I exhale and stamp out the one I've got. Then the two of us light up a new Stuyve each.

I've decided to let my hair grow, and that's the first thing she picks on. She points at her own head. You're one of those guys, aren't you, she says.

Esona's smile is slight, showing only half of its bow behind the smoke.

You grow your hair out like a Rasta, she says, but stand first in line for meat at the bash. Okay, she tells me, I see.

Then she turns around and shows me the other half of her smile.

She says, so what's your deal, my brother?

I'm not sure how to respond. Esona takes off her backpack and asks me for the time, but when I look down at my wrist, I realize I've left my wristwatch in Obs. This reminds me of what Cecelia used to say to me about my listening.

I don't know, I tell Esona.

And I guess this is how she enters my life.

What's your deal, my brother?

She'll ask me that often.

These days, I don't think about Last Life as much as I used

to, but I think about the things I'll remember when it's time for me to go.

I think of Esona's flesh a lot.

I think of the sticky underside of her breasts when I lift them to my face in the middle of summer, and I think of the smell of burning wood, and of Esona's last name, Grootboom, and how her grandmother took it to pass them off as coloreds in '78.

I think of our hair, too, the way the smell of coal still lingers on our necks and up our heads for a day after sitting on the dirty benches of a *shisa nyama*. I think of all the sticky vinyl under the J&B ashtrays we fill up at the local taverns.

I want you to fuck me like a new man, she tells me.

She's standing behind me in the kitchen, looking for a lighter, and I'm on my feet, trying to tune a new station into their old set.

Esona lives in a two-room with her aunt in Slovo. Her mother's a nurse, stationed across the country and I guess growing old there. For most of her life, that's how it's been between them. First there were nightshifts at Grey Hospital in King William's Town, and then there was the move to Fort Beaufort, and then another to Grahamstown, and now she's moored in Stutterheim. Sometimes, when Esona speaks, I try to imagine her mother. I see a woman with Esona's face, her sleeves rolled up, creasing her brow in a ward full of crying children. Or maybe that's Sis' Thobeka. In any case, neither of them is around enough to see what we do on the floors here, so I guess it's okay that my shirt and her panties already lie inside the fruit bowl on the coffee table.

I've been back a week since my initiation in eMthatha.

I went over to Luthando's grave when my family was finally done with me. It was a clear day and I didn't say much to him, down there. We never had to use words to discover an understanding between us.

I guess a lot has happened since then. I waved on my way out, and I said, later, Luthando, and that was about it.

Later, Luthando.

Now I lie stretched out on Esona's cold kitchen floor.

I disclosed my status to her just a day after we'd met and we've worshiped at the altar of her caution ever since. Esona gets me to bring our condoms back from Sis' Thoko's shop.

I watch her now as she looks at the inflated flesh around the tip of my penis, still tender from my journey back home. She handles me with caution between her long, thin fingers, and her nails tickle my underside like the tip of an ivy leaf. Then she pushes her teeth into me and puts a hand on my chest when I begin to stir. For a long time, I just lie there, on the brink of screaming, and then I feel surprise when even this pain dissipates. On her knees on the kitchen floor, Esona releases me, grips my scrotum, and squeezes it before I melt and empty myself on her chest. Later, I fall asleep to the feel of her salt water drying on my face, and sleeping beside me, she breathes her air out as hot as a furnace, and I close my eyes; but this time, unlike so many others in my life, I don't clench them.

Bhut' Vuyo never explicitly reminds me of my promise, but I remember and live through it each day. My promise, what I told them then, is the same thing I'll tell you now. My name, which my parents got from a girl, is Lindanathi. It means wait with us, and that's what I plan on doing. So in the end, I guess this is to you, Luthando. This is your older brother, Lindanathi, and I'm ready to react for us.

SQUARE WAVE A NOVEL BY MARK DE SILVA

"Brilliant." —*3:AM Magazine*

"Enticing and enthralling, [*Square Wave*] aims to hit all the literary neurons. This might be the closest we get to David Mitchell on LSD. *Square Wave* is the perfect concoction for the thirsty mind." —*Atticus Review*

NOTHING A NOVEL BY ANNE MARIE WIRTH CAUCHON

"Apocalyptic and psychologically attentive. I was moved." —*New York Times Book Review*

"A riveting first piece of scripture from our newest prophet of misspent youth." —*Paste*

THE VISITING SUIT A NOVEL BY XIAODA XIAO

"[Xiao] recount[s] his struggle in sometimes unexpectedly lovely detail. Against great odds, in the grimmest of settings, he manages to find good in the darkness." —*New York Times Book Review*

"These stories personify the compassion, humor, and dignity inherent not just in survival but in triumphing over despair." —*O, The Oprah Magazine*

I'M TRYING TO REACH YOU
A NOVEL BY BARBARA BROWNING

* *The Believer* Book Award Finalist

"I think I love this book so much because it contains intimations of the potential of what books can be in the future, and also because it's hilarious." —Emily Gould, *BuzzFeed*

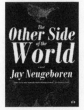

THE OTHER SIDE OF THE WORLD
A NOVEL BY JAY NEUGEBOREN

"Epic… *The Other Side of the World* can charm you with its grace, intelligence, and scope… [An] inventive novel." —*Washington Post*

"Presents a meditation on life, love, art, and family relationships that's reminiscent of the best of John Updike." —*Kirkus Reviews* (starred)

THE GLACIER A NOVEL BY JEFF WOOD

"Gorgeously and urgently written." —*Library Journal* (starred)

"It seduces you slowly, the reader hypnotized from the first page."
—*Heavy Feather Review*

"An innovatively told book, a truly cinematic novel." —Largehearted Boy

THE ONLY ONES A NOVEL BY CAROLA DIBBELL

* **One of the Best Books of 2015** —*O, The Oprah Magazine, Washington Post, Flavorwire, National Post*

"Breathtaking. It's that good, and that important, and that heartbreakingly beautiful." —NPR

"A heart-piercing tale of love, desire, and acceptance." —*Washington Post*

HAINTS STAY A NOVEL BY COLIN WINNETTE

* **One of the Best Books of 2015** —*Slate, Flavorwire*

"[An] astonishing portrait of American violence. The rewards of *Haints Stay* belong to the reader." —*Los Angeles Times*

"A success… *Haints Stay* turns the Western on its ear." —*Washington Post*

SOME THINGS THAT MEANT THE WORLD TO ME
A NOVEL BY JOSHUA MOHR

* ***San Francisco Chronicle* Bestseller**
* **One of the Best Books of 2009** —*O, The Oprah Magazine, The Nervous Breakdown*

"Mohr's prose roams with chimerical liquidity." —Boston's *Weekly Dig*

THE CORRESPONDENCE ARTIST
A NOVEL BY BARBARA BROWNING

* **Lambda Literary Award Winner**

"A deft look at modern life that's both witty and devastating." —*Nylon*

"*The Correspondence Artist* applies stylistic juxtapositions in welcome and unexpected ways." —*Vol. 1 Brooklyn*

Also published by **Two Dollar Radio**

Visit TwoDollarRadio.com for 25% off, bundle sales, and more!

CRYSTAL EATERS A NOVEL BY SHANE JONES

"A powerful narrative that touches on the value of every human life, with a lyrical voice and layers of imagery and epiphany." —*BuzzFeed*

"[Jones is] something of a millennial Richard Brautigan." —*Nylon*

"A mythical and hallucinatory experience of a family fighting mortality." —Publishers Weekly

HOW TO GET INTO THE TWIN PALMS
A NOVEL BY KAROLINA WACLAWIAK

"One of my favorite books this year." —Roxane Gay, *The Rumpus*

"Waclawiak's novel reinvents the immigration story." —*New York Times Book Review*, Editors' Choice

CRAPALACHIA A NOVEL BY SCOTT McCLANAHAN

 * **One of the Best Books of 2013** —*The Millions, Flavorwire, Dazed & Confused, The L Magazine, Time Out Chicago*

"McClanahan's prose is miasmic, dizzying, repetitive. A rushing river of words that reflects the chaos and humanity of the place from which he hails." —*New York Times Book Review*

NOT DARK YET A NOVEL BY BERIT ELLINGSEN

"Fascinating, surreal, gorgeously written, and like nothing you've ever read before." —*BuzzFeed*

"… suspenseful and haunting… This is a remarkable novel from a very talented author." —*Publishers Weekly* (starred)

MIRA CORPORA A NOVEL BY JEFF JACKSON

 * *Los Angeles Times* **Book Prize Finalist**
 * **One of the Best Books of 2013** —*Slate, Salon, Flavorwire*

"Style is pre-eminent in Jeff Jackson's eerie and enigmatic debut. The prose works like the expressionless masks worn by killers in horror films." —*Wall Street Journal*

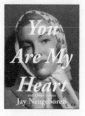

I SMILE BACK A NOVEL BY AMY KOPPELMAN

* Now a major film starring Sarah Silverman & Josh Charles!

"Powerful. Koppelman's instincts help her navigate these choppy waters with inventiveness and integrity." —*Los Angeles Times*

"Koppelman explores with ruthless honesty a woman come undone." —*Bookslut*

ANCIENT OCEANS OF CENTRAL KENTUCKY
A NOVEL BY DAVID CONNERLEY NAHM

* One of the Best Books of 2014 —NPR, *Flavorwire*

"Wonderful… Remarkable… it's impossible to stop reading until you've gone through each beautiful line, a beauty that infuses the whole novel, even in its darkest moments." —*NPR*

THE PEOPLE WHO WATCHED HER PASS BY
A NOVEL BY SCOTT BRADFIELD

"Challenging [and] original… A billowy adventure of a book. In a book that supplies few answers, Bradfield's lavish eloquence is the presiding constant." —*New York Times Book Review*

"Brave and unforgettable." —*Los Angeles Times*

1940 A NOVEL BY JAY NEUGEBOREN

"Jay Neugeboren traverses the Hitlerian tightrope with all the skill and formal daring that have made him one of our most honored writers of literary fiction and masterful nonfiction. [*1940*] is, at once, a beautifully realized work of imagined history, a rich and varied character study and a subtly layered novel of ideas, all wrapped in a propulsively readable story." —*Los Angeles Times*

BABY GEISHA STORIES BY TRINIE DALTON

"[The stories] feel like brilliant sexual fairy tales on drugs. Dalton writes of self-discovery and sex with a knowing humility and humor." —*Interview Magazine*

"Dalton handles her narratives with a deft skill and a keen, distinct, confident voice that never eases up." —*The Brooklyn Rail*

Also published by *Two Dollar Radio*

Visit TwoDollarRadio.com for 25% off, bundle sales, and more!

THE CAVE MAN A NOVEL BY XIAODA XIAO

* WOSU (NPR member station) Favorite Book of 2009

"As a parable of modern China, [*The Cave Man*] is chilling."
—*Boston Globe*

"Hair-raising. Xiao's literary ancestors include Kafka and Solzhenitsyn."
—*Counterpunch*

SEVEN DAYS IN RIO A NOVEL BY FRANCIS LEVY

"The funniest American novel since Sam Lipsyte's *The Ask*."
—*Village Voice*

"Like an erotic version of Luis Bunuel's *The Discreet Charm of the Bourgeoisie*." —*The Cult*

THE DROP EDGE OF YONDER
A NOVEL BY RUDOLPH WURLITZER

* *Time Out New York*'s Best Book of 2008
* *ForeWord Magazine* 2008 Gold Medal in Literary Fiction

"A picaresque American *Book of the Dead*... in the tradition of Thomas Pynchon, Joseph Heller, Kurt Vonnegut, and Terry Southern."
—*Los Angeles Times*

THE SHANGHAI GESTURE
A NOVEL BY GARY INDIANA

"An uproarious, confounding, turbocharged fantasia that manages, alongside all its imaginative bravura, to hold up to our globalized epoch the fun-house mirror it deserves." —*Bookforum*

"Funny, in something of the parodic, tongue-in-cheek mode of *The Princess Bride* or *Austin Powers*." —*Washington Post*

TERMITE PARADE A NOVEL BY JOSHUA MOHR

* *Sacramento Bee* Best Read of 2010

"[A] wry and unnerving story of bad love gone rotten. [Mohr] has a generous understanding of his characters, whom he describes with an intelligence and sensitivity that pulls you in. This is no small achievement."
—*New York Times Book Review*

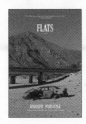
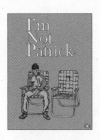